Child of the Wilderness

A Young Boy's Courage

Alan Swope

iUniverse LLC
Bloomington

CHILD OF THE WILDERNESS
A Young Boy's Courage

This is a work of fiction. All of the characters, names, incidents, organizations, and dialogue in this novel are either the products of the author's imagination or are used fictitiously.

iUniverse books may be ordered through booksellers or by contacting:

iUniverse LLC
1663 Liberty Drive
Bloomington, IN 47403
www.iuniverse.com
1-800-Authors (1-800-288-4677)

Because of the dynamic nature of the Internet, any web addresses or links contained in this book may have changed since publication and may no longer be valid. The views expressed in this work are solely those of the author and do not necessarily reflect the views of the publisher, and the publisher hereby disclaims any responsibility for them.

Any people depicted in stock imagery provided by Thinkstock are models, and such images are being used for illustrative purposes only. Certain stock imagery © Thinkstock.

ISBN: 978-1-4917-1053-1 (sc)
ISBN: 978-1-4917-1055-5 (hc)
ISBN: 978-1-4917-1054-8 (e)

Printed in the United States of America.

iUniverse rev. date: 11/22/2013

Prologue

The Shannon family, Frank, Eileen and their two children Jimmy ten and Jodie seven, lived in Memphis Tennessee. Frank was a new car salesman, business was slow he barely made enough money to support his family.

Eileen had often talked to Frank about her finding a job to help with the finances but Frank was against it, "Eileen, we have talked about this many times someone has to be here to take care of the house and children." "And that someone is me!" she would answer. With that said Eileen's anger would flare up, she would be mad at Frank, raising her voice when she talked to him which would make him mad, then the argument started. They would argue about things that they argued about before in the past.

When Jimmy and Jodie heard them, they would try to hide because they knew when this happened their parents would take it out on them, by way of some kind of punishment. Frank would find some reason to spank Jimmy and Eileen would scold Jodie for no reason. Jimmy and Jodie would often talk about how mean their parents were to them, that's why when the argument started they would try to hide to no avail.

It was spring now and this past winter wasn't any better as far as business was concerned. It was Thursday midmorning when Frank saw a man and women looking at a new car, he approached them he introduced himself. They in turn introduced themselves as Mr. and Mrs. Norton, and they had been on vacation and was heading home when their car started acting up. Besides selling Mr. and Mrs. Norton a new car, Frank found out that they owned a huge warehouse in Billings Montana that stored and shipped merchandise to the western half of the U.S. and south western Canada. Sometimes if the order was big enough they would ship to the Midwest. Also during their conversation Frank learned that they were looking for a shipping manager.

Frank asked if he could have the job, that he had experience in shipping merchandise and he was in charge of shipping used cars to different places around the country when other car dealers or used car lots needed a particular car for a customer. Mr. Norton gave Frank the job, said he could start in two weeks after he settled his affairs there in Memphis. Eileen wasn't crazy about moving to Billings but Frank agreed she could find a job if she wished to do so. Eileen's parents also lived in Memphis, they said they would take care of the selling of their house. Two weeks later the Shannon family was in Billings Montana, rented a house and Frank was back to work as the new shipping manager at Norton Warehouse INC.

Eileen found a job as hostess in a fancy restaurant in town, Frank earned a lot more money and Eileen's income went a long way in helping to make ends meet. Things were finally looking up.

Chapter One

On Saturday July 3, 1975, a day before Jimmy's 10th birthday the family had just sat down at the table for lunch when the phone rang. Frank got up to answer it, picking up the receiver he said "Hello" then he listened for a few minutes before saying . . . "Give me an hour and a half, we're just having lunch, I'll be there as soon as I can." then he hung up the phone, went back to his chair, looking at Eileen, he said "That was Dave Hanson, he said there are six items that has to be loaded on the truck going to Seattle. They can't find the items or the paperwork he wanted to know if I knew where they were. I remember seeing the bill of lading, but don't remember which aisle they were put in. I'll have to go down and look for them, it shouldn't take long. Dave said these items have to go."

"Okay, you go take care of that, I have some cleaning to do and the laundry." After his mother stopped talking, Jimmy spoke up . . . "Dad, can I go with you?" Frank looked at his son . . . "Jimmy, I'm only going to be gone a couple of hours." "I know," said Jimmy "I can help you look." Frank seeing the look on his son's face, and the excitement in his voice, he decided to let his son go with him. "Okay son, you can come with me, but you will have to stay with me, I don't want you wondering around. They will be unloading trucks it will be very busy you could get hurt." "I will." Jimmy said "I won't wonder."

Arriving at the warehouse, Frank parked close to the front entrance he and Jimmy went in through the front door to the main lobby then through the door to the right of the lobby, past the other offices and into the warehouse. It was set up with row after row after row of shelves

1

stacked five high, all the rows of shelving was framed together with medal bars with notches cut in them, they were the vertical frame work, the horizontal bars had tabs on each end that fit into the notches. They all had two by six boards on the bars for the pallets to sit on. Each space between the vertical uprights could hold three pallets. As Frank and Jimmy were walking through the warehouse toward the receiving office, Frank would say hi to those he knew, a few times he would stop to talk for a few minutes, he would ask that person if he or she knew if the six items had been found. The ones he talked to said they didn't know.

Frank and Jimmy made their way to the receiving office, dodging or waiting for forklifts to pass them as they went in and out of trucks, inside the office, Frank sat in the chair at his desk Jimmy sat in a chair in front of the desk. Picking up the phone, Frank called the shipping office which was on the other side of the building, when answered he asked for Dave, he was told that Dave was on the floor looking for the six items.

"Find Dave and tell him I am in my office, and to bring whatever paperwork he has on those items." Frank said, "I'll need that paperwork to look up the shipping and receiving numbers." While Frank was waiting for Dave, he went through all the paperwork in the incoming and outgoing bins on his desk, not knowing what he was looking for he thought to himself, 'This is stupid, I'll wait for Dave.' He got up and went to the coffee pot in the corner, picking up the half empty pot he smelled the coffee, it seemed fresh so he poured a cup. As he was putting the pot down, Dave walked in. They greeted each other, Dave handed him the paperwork one sheet of paper. "Sorry to call you in on your day off," said Dave, "But we do have to find those six items." "Want some coffee Dave?" Frank asked. "No thanks Frank." They both went to Frank's desk, "Dave, this is my son Jimmy." Dave and Jimmy shook hands. "Glad to meet you Jimmy." And Jimmy replied . . . "I'm happy to meet you to sir."

Frank looked at the sheet of paper Dave gave him, the names of the items, and a few numbers, then, he started looking through all the papers on his desk. Not finding what he was looking for, he went to the filing cabinet and started looking through the folder marked shipped and the folder marked received, still not finding it, he then looked through the pending file, and found the paperwork at the bottom of the pile. Pulling out the original bill of lading, Frank looked at it, at the bottom of the page was written aisle twenty three in pink highlight, "No wonder you couldn't find them, they're not suppose too be in that aisle. This kind of merchandise goes in aisle seventy two." Frank said handing the paperwork to Dave.

"I'll have one of my men pick them up and load them on the truck, thanks Frank again I'm sorry to call you in on your day off." "Not a problem Dave," Frank said, "I'm glad we got this mystery solved, by the way, I heard you and Alice are expecting again."

"Yes we are, this will be our second I hope it's a girl, Alice wants a boy and Jason wants a little sister." "Why, another boy?" Frank asked. "Alice said boys are a lot easier than girls growing up. You don't have to worry as much when they are teenagers you know how kids are today you never know what they are up to." Dave commented. "That's true, are you going to find out if it's a boy or girl before its born?" Frank asked. "I don't know, we talked about it but haven't decided yet. I am in favor of it, Alice said she would think it over and let me know when she decides." Dave said. "It would be nice to know, you can make plans for a nursery and decide on a name, but then again it is always a thrill to find out when the baby is born." Frank replied. "I know, either way I will be just as proud, thanks Frank, I have to get back to work."

Frank stayed in his office for another half hour going thru papers and straightening up his desk, he filed some papers, put some in the outgoing box, some in the pending file. No one had come in for coffee so he turned the pot off. When he was satisfied the way the office looked, he decided it was time to go home.

You're going home now?" A lady on a fork lift asked. "Yes, Jimmy and I will be leaving the family has plans for this afternoon." "Well then Mr. Shannon, I'll see you on Monday." Frank and Jimmy left the office heading for the main lobby when Mr. Norton the general manager called his name they walked out of the building onto the dock. While the manager and Frank were talking Jimmy asked where the restroom was, his dad pointed to it, both restrooms were along the wall, to the right of the main lobby door, Jimmy started walking that way, he noticed some plaques on the wall, as he got to them he stopped to read each one.

The plaques were about 'Employee of the month' with a picture at the top and the name of the employee on a gold plate in the middle, at the bottom of the plaque was a real solid gold medallion the size of a silver dollar. Jimmy read each one, the last one was near the door to the men's room, while Jimmy was reading it his father and the manager was watching him. They both turned away when there was a loud noise behind them. Two-ten foot long pipes had rolled off the pallet that was being loaded.

When Jimmy returned, he, and his dad left, arriving at home, Frank parked the car in the garage. Entering the house, Eileen and Jodie was sitting at the kitchen table "What's the matter?" Frank asked when he saw Jodie holding a wet cloth to her forehead, "Jodie isn't feeling well, she has a temperature of one hundred and one all plans are off for this weekend." Eileen said. "I am putting herto bed, I'm going to keep a close eye on her if she gets worse I will take her to the doctor."

Jodie was put to bed, Eileen got a small pot, she put some ice and water in it, grabbed a cloth and the phone and went up to Jodie's room, dipping the cloth in icy water then wringing out the cloth she placed it on Jodie's forehead. Sitting on the edge of the bed Eileen dialed the number for the hospital, when the nurse answered Eileen told her about Jodie and about putting the cold cloth on Jodie's forehead and asked what she should do, short of bringing her in. The nurse told her to keep putting the cold cloth on her, and take her temperature every 15 minutes, to make sure she writes down the time and temperature, if she gets any worse to bring her in. Jimmy was standing at the door watching, he heard what his mother said, when she put the phone down, Jimmy said . . . "Mom, I will put the cold cloth on Jodie if you have something else to do." "Thanks Jimmy, I do have to get dinner ready, I'll be back in a few minutes."

Jimmy sat on the edge of the bed and did what his mother did, dipping the cloth in the cold water and placing it on Jodie's forehead, while he was doing this he talked to her, "Don't worry sis, you'll be alright, we all get sick." About 15 minutes later, Eileen came in and felt Jodie's forehead, it seemed to be cooler. "I am making some soup for you, it will be ready in a few minutes, Jimmy, dinner is ready, Jodie, I am going to eat first, then I will bring you your soup and take your temperature again, come along Jimmy."

After dinner, Eileen took a bowl of soup up to Jodie and Frank went into the front room, turned on the TV and sat in his recliner, he turned to the weather channel. Jimmy cleared the table, put the dishes in the dish washer then went to his room he closed the door and started playing with his toys. Eileen fed Jodie, then took her temperature and wrote in down, her temperature had dropped, it was now 99, she took the pot to get some more ice and water, while she was in the kitchen she noticed it had been cleaned up. The phone rang, and she answered it . . . "Hello"

"Mrs. Shannon, this is Mr. Norton, may I speak to Frank please?" "Yes, of course Mr. Norton, I'll get him." laying the phone down, she picked up the pot of ice water and headed for the stairs, she stopped at the foot and said to Frank . . . "Frank, the phone is for you, it's Mr. Norton." Frank got up from his chair and walking past the stairs he said . . . "Looks like rain this weekend, starts tonight through Monday." his wife didn't answer, she disappeared into Jodie's room.

"Mom, is it going to rain, with lightning and thunder, and everything?" Jodie asked, "I don't like thunder and lightning." "That's what your father said, but you don't have to worry about the thunder and lightning, you are not outside so the lightning won't hurt you and the thunder is only a loud noise and as the storm moves away the thunder become more distant and quiet, then there is only rain." "I don't mind just rain," Jodie said, "I can go to sleep listening to the rain." Eileen smiled at her while Jodie was eating, "So can I sweetheart, the rain has a soothing sound, and it is easy to fall asleep listening to it." "Is it going to rain tomorrow too?" asked Jodie. "Your father said it might rain tomorrow and the next day." "Where's Jimmy?" Jodie asked. "He's in his room, playing with his toys, why?" "I would like to talk to him, will you tell him I want to talk to him?" "Yes dear, do you want some more soup?" Jodie shook her head no.

Eileen got up and told her to rest, she went to Jimmy's room and told him that Jodie wanted to see him. They both went to Jodie's room Jimmy sat on the bed while Eileen stood. "Jimmy, I'm afraid of the lightning and thunder, will you stay with me?" "Yes sis I will stay with you, but you don't have to be afraid, they won't hurt you." Jimmy said. Just at that moment there was a flash of light outside, it wasn't very bright, a few seconds later there was a loud crackling noise then a loud boom as the thunder rumbled across the sky and over the mountain tops and through the valleys. It was enough to make Jodie cover her head.

"Jodie," Jimmy said . . . "I read in a book, that when you see lightning, you should count one thousand one, one thousand two, and so on then went you hear thunder that will tell you how many miles away the storm is, I counted this one, and the storm is five miles away. As it gets closer, the lightning will flash brighter and the thunder will boom louder sooner, We don't have to worry about any of that cause we're inside, the thunder only makes a loud noise, so I will stay with you so you won't be scared, okay?" "Okay," she said.

"I'll be right back I have to put my toys away," "Please don't be long Jimmy I want you to stay with me till the storm goes away!""Okay sis, I'll hurry." Jimmy left her room and Eileen went down stairs. He knew his sister was scared so he hurried, putting all his toys away except one, it was a small black horse, a stuffed animal, Jodie liked horses, she always said horses were strong, and protected its owner, he figured it might help calm her down, he made up his mind, he would stay with her all night if he had to. Jimmy and Jodie loved each other as brother and sister. To her, Jimmy was always her big brother who protected her, who looked after her.

One of the main reasons Jodie looked up to Jimmy is because he is like many boys across the country that have younger sisters. They will fight to protect their sister if they have to, that's just what Jimmy did one day after school. It happened last year, Jimmy was in second grade, Jodie was in kindergarten, the day he fought for Jodie, (well it really can't be called a fight) a boy named Buster Simmons was a bully, he always picked on boys smaller than he, or sometimes he would pick on girls, this day he was picking on Jodie, poking her, yanking on her hair, and calling her a little sissy, he made Jodie cry, when Jimmy saw what he was doing and Jodie crying, it made him mad. He didn't say a word, with his hand doubled into a fist he just walked up to Buster and punched him as hard as he could.

The swing was a straight thru punch directly at his nose, it connected square in the middle of the buster's face and the blow knocked him down, his nose was bleeding, his eyes filled with tears and he started crying, Jimmy stood over him, he put one foot on his chest, pointed his index finger at him and said, "Jodie is my sister, if I ever see you bothering her again, or hear you bothered her, I will come after you and I won't stop here, it will be a lot worse, now get up and get out of here."

He faced the bully till he got up and ran off crying, the other kids that was there yelled and cheered, "Yeah Jimmy!" he walked over to Jodie and hugged her, "You okay sis?" he asked. She looked up at him, tears running down her face, he gently wiped them away, "Yes . . . I . . . I'm okay, my head hurts where he pull . . . pulled my hair!" Jimmy very gently, kept wiping her tears away, finally she stopped crying. "He won't bother you anymore!" Jimmy told her. "Are you sure? I don't like him, he's mean." "Yes, I'm sure, I will talk to him tomorrow and let him know he is not to bother you or even talk to you again, it will be okay."

The incident happened on the school ground, the teachers and parents that were there didn't see it happen but when the other kids cheered Jimmy they looked in that direction, a group of kids like that cheering meant only one thing, A FIGHT. Two of the teachers started that way when they saw buster running toward them, he was crying, his nose was bleeding, and the blood was running into his mouth and down his chin and onto his shirt. One of the teachers stopped him and asked what happened. "JI . . . JI . . . Jimmy pun . . . punched me!" "Why would Jimmy punch you?" asked the teacher. "I . . . I . . . don't know!" Buster answered. "You wait here, I'll go find out!" The teacher, Mr. Thomas Bigelow went over to the group of kids, seeing Jimmy, he asked him what happened.

Jimmy explained what he saw Buster doing to Jodie and it made him mad, so he hit Buster to protect his sister. All of the other kids spoke up and agreed with Jimmy, they said they saw what Buster was doing to Jodie, but was scared to try to stop him, they all said he's a bully, that he always picks on boys who are smaller than he is or he picks on girls. Mr. Bigelow told them to go to their bus or to where their parents were to pick them up. He went back to where Buster was waiting, "Come with me Buster." Mr. Bigelow took Buster into the Principals office and told him to have a seat, then told the principal, Mrs. Nancy Stoddard what Buster had said then what all the other kids said. "Thank you, Mr. Bigelow I will handle it from here."

After Mr. Bigelow left, Mrs. Stoddard looked at Buster "Well Buster Simmons what do you have to say for yourself?" Buster just sat there, he didn't say a word. "Well Buster, by your silence, I would say you started it, you were picking on Jodie, weren't you?" She got up and got him a tissue to wipe the blood off his face, then sat back down, "Well Buster?" "I wasn't picking on Jodie, I was just having fun." buster answered. "That isn't what I would call fun," Mrs. Stoddard said in anger, "It is what I would call mean, you have been told about this before, I have no choice but to call your mother and tell her to come get you, and that you are being suspended for one month, you will have to make up that one month at the end of the year. You will sit right there till your mother gets here."

"You don't have to call my mother," buster said, "She's not home anyway, we don't live far, I can walk home!" "I'm not letting you walk home, so please just sit there and be quiet." Mrs. Stoddard looked up the number then dialed, when the phone was answered she said, "Hello, Mrs. Simmons, this is Mrs. Stoddard, Buster's school principle, Buster got into trouble again today, I need you to come to my office, Buster is here and he will stay here till you pick him up, also I need to talk to you." "I see, very well Mrs. Stoddard, I'm just finishing something here in the house I'll be there in half an hour will that be alright?" "Yes Mrs. Simmons, that will be fine see you then."

Mrs. Simmons arrived at Buster's elementary school in the outer office she told the secretary that Mrs. Stoddard wanted to see her. She was told to go right, Mrs. Stoddard was expecting her, Mrs. Simmons knocked on the door then went in, seeing Buster sitting in a chair in front of her desk, she sat down in the chair beside him, looking at her son, she saw the blood on his face and asked him, "Buster, what happened to you?" In response he said, "A boy hit me!" "Why, what did you do?" "I didn't do anything he just hit me for no reason." Mrs. Simmons looked at Mrs. Stoddard, "Can you tell me what happened?"

"Yes Mrs. Simmons, I can, Your son Buster here, after his last class was picking on a kindergarten girl, pulling her hair, poking her and calling her names. The girls brother who is in Busters class, saw what he was doing, he then walked up to Buster and punched him in the nose." "What happened to the other boy? Where is he?" Mrs. Simmons asked. "Nothing happened to the other boy he isn't being punished he was defending his sister, MR. Biga . . . ." "What do you mean nothing happened to the other boy," Mrs. Simmons said starting to get angry. "He punched Buster and you are not going to punish him?"

"No, Mrs. Simmons, I'm not, and I'll tell you why, your son Buster here is a bully, he picks on boys smaller than him also little girls, he said it is fun for him, this is not the first time this has happened, he has been here in my office four times since school started, I have warned him each time, it doesn't seem to do any good. This is the fifth time, so now I am going to do something about it. I had hoped I wouldn't have to do this . . . , I am expelling him for one month Buster can make up that one month at the end of the school year.

"Your expelling him, I hope you have good reason, I can take you to court you know!" "Yes, I am expelling him for one month, and yes I know you can take me to court. But let me tell you something else, your son is a liar, he told me not to call you because you weren't home, and I have caught him in other lies to. These are my reasons, so if you want to take me to court, go ahead, now you can take Buster home, so if you will excuse me I have work to do."

Outside, walking to the car, Mrs. Simmons looked at Buster, "What is wrong with you, your always getting into trouble, if you are going to pick on the other kids, pick on someone your own age and size." "I don't want to do that, they might beat me up!" he said. "Maybe that's what you need, someone to beat the crap out of you." "You wouldn't care," he said, "Your always working or going out with some man, you never take time for me.

Mrs. Simmons thought about that, "I have to make a living for us you know your dad is a bum and an alcoholic, he left us two years ago." "Yeah, and you two was fighting all the time, I didn't like that, and you have all those tatoo'son your body, their ugly!" "How do you know about my tatoo's?" "I've seen them." "When" asked Mrs. Simmons. "MOOOM, after you shower, you run around the house in your house coat, and it doesn't stay closed, think about it!" "Buster, your only ten, you are not suppose too see things like that." "Well I do, I would like you to spend more time with me, we can do fun things, play games, take walks, read to each other, I need to read better, you could help me with my homework, sometimes we could just sit and talk, talk about anything, I would like that you know." "You mean I could be a better mom!" "It wouldn't hurt you." Buster said with tears in his eyes.

Chapter Two

Frank picked up the phone from the counter and said . . . "Hello Mr. Norton, how may I help you?" "Afternoon Frank, sorry to bother you, but something came up this afternoon, when you and your son were here, you and I talked on the dock and your son Jimmy asked where the restroom was, you and I watched him while we were talking and he stopped to read the plaques on the wall." "Yes sir, I remember, is there anything wrong with that?"

"No Frank, what's wrong is the last plaque, next to the men's room, the solid gold medallion is missing, I'm not saying your son took it, but he was the last person near those plaques, he even took time to read them. Now Frank, please don't misunderstand me, I'm not accusing Jimmy, what I'm saying is, he was the last one near them that I know of." "Yes sir, I will talk to Jimmy about this. Do you want me to call you back after I talk to him?" "No Frank, enjoy your weekend, we can talk on Monday."

When Frank hung up the phone, he went to the foot of the stairs and yelled . . . "EILEEN . . . EILEEN," When she appeared at the top of the stairs she yelled, "WHAT?" "Tell Jimmy I want to see him down here immediately." "What's wrong?" she asked. "You'll find out when I talk to him, just bring him down here." When Jimmy and Eileen came down stairs, they went into the front room they saw Frank pacing back and forth with an angry look on his face. Frank looked at Jimmy then said very angrily . . . "Sit down in that chair young man and don't say anything till I'm thru talking. Do you understand?"

"What's wrong?" Eileen asked. Frank looked at his wife. "Mr. Norton told me on the phone, that the solid gold medallion on the last plaque next to the men's room is missing. He said he wasn't accusing Jimmy, but he was the last person to look at them." Frank turned to look at his son . . . "Now Jimmy, I want you to be honest with me . . . did you take the gold coin off that plaque you were looking at?" "No dad, I didn't, I was just looking at them." Frank just stood there studying his son when Eileen said . . . Jimmy we want the truth, you know we don't hold with lying or stealing. Now, you tell us what happened." "Nothing happened I was just looking at them that's all." "DON'T LIE TO US," Frank yelled . . . "You took that gold medallion didn't you?" "NO" Jimmy yelled back. Out of reflex from being upset over this, his mother slapped him. "Don't you dare lie too me!"

Jimmy started crying, he jumped up from the chair and ran to the bottom of the stairs, he stopped, looked at them and said . . . "I'm not lying, and I'm leaving because you don't believe me, I won't stay where I'm not wanted. He then ran up the stairs to his room. His mom and dad didn't worry about him leaving he had done this same thing a few times before only under different circumstances. Jimmy would pack a bag, go out the front door and walk around to the back patio he would just sit there for a while then go in the house.

Up in his room Jimmy got his back pack, dumped everything out of it, then he started putting what he wanted into it, when he was done, he changed shoes to his work type boots, picked up his back pack and went into Jodie's room, "How do you feel sis?" "I'm okay I feel a lot better, where are you going?" "I'm leaving. Mom and dad think I stole a gold coin today from where dad works. I didn't. They don't believe me." Jimmy told her.

"Mom told me not to lie to them, then she slapped me, I'm okay. I wanted to say good-by. I'll see you again sometime." "Jimmy, your only nine, what will you do, where will you go?" "I'll be ten tomorrow, I don't know where I'll go, I just can't stay here with them not believing me. We both know how mean dad is sometimes, I know I will miss you." He said. "I will miss you too, give me a hug good-by." She said with tears in her eyes.

Jimmy and Jodie hugged each other, then he kissed her on the cheek, and she in turn kissed him on the cheek. "Take good care of yourself . . . , and be careful around mom and dad. You know how mean they are to us." "Bye Jimmy, try to let me know where you are, if you can." "I will." Jimmy left her room and went down stairs, he was heading for the front door when his dad said . . . "Hold it right there young man, I want to check your backpack!" Jimmy handed it to his dad, and his dad opened it and dumped everything on the floor, going thru everything he said . . . "Two pair of sox, two shirts, two pair of pants, a pocket knife, a small ball of twine, a ball of string, two pair of underwear, and a pair of tennis shoes, a hat, a winter coat and a rain coat, but no medallion." Frank searched every pocket on Jimmy's pants and shirt. "When you leave, your mother and I will search your room." "Go ahead, I don't care." Said Jimmy with a tear sliding down his cheek.

Frank said . . . "It's all yours you can repack everything and leave. After Jimmy had everything put back into his pack, he reached for the door knob opening the door his mother said . . . "Write when you can." He looked at both of them but didn't say a word. He walked outside closing the door behind him. Frank went back into the front room to his recliner. Eileen went upstairs to check on Jodie. She noticed that Jodie had been putting the cold cloth on her forehead. "Let me check your temperature." she said, "Wow, your fever is down. It's at 98.6, normal do you feel like getting up?" "No mom, I'm going to stay here, I am hungry. Could you bring me something?" "Yes dear, I'll be right back."

In the kitchen Eileen was fixing Jodie a sandwich, she told Frank that Jodie's temperature was back to normal. She looked out the window, but didn't see Jimmy anywhere, she then went to check the back patio, no Jimmy, she started to worry, she, went outside and walked all around the house, still no Jimmy. Back inside she told Frank she was worried, he said that Jimmy was hiding somewhere, not to worry, when it gets dark he will be coming in, he always does. The clouds were building up over the western mountains and were real dark," It's going to rain soon," she said, "I hope he comes in soon." Eileen went to one of the front room windows and looked out toward the west, as she stared at the mountains her mind was running wild with all kinds of thoughts about her son. She was worried. 'Where is he, why won't he come in, he knows it will rain soon. Where could he have went, I wish now that I hadn't slapped him. I bet he is blaming me, he told us the truth about that stupid medallion, why didn't I believe him. Jimmy, please come home.' Thoughts filled her eyes with tears.

That evening after Jodie ate, she stayed in her room, she, didn't want to be around her parents that night. The rain had started and it was coming down hard, the wind was blowing and seemed to be howling, still

Jimmy had not come in. It was 6:15 when the phone rang, Frank reached over picked up the receiver "Hello" "Frank, Pete Norton here, I thought I had better call you to let you know that we found the gold medallion. Miss Norma Johnson came to me and told me she saw Hank Short use a knife to pop the medallion off the plaque. Dave Hanson and I called Hank into the receiving office and confronted him. We told him that we know he took it.

He finally admitted it and gave it back. I fired him right then, he no longer works here, I know he is one of your men. Sorry but you will be one man short for a while." "That's good Mr. Norton, I'm glad you recovered the medallion, we don't need men like Mr. Short, I can handle it without him, OHHH MY GOD, I talked to Jimmy this afternoon and accused him of taking the medallion, we had a little argument and he left home."

"What . . . ! What do you mean he left home?" "Just that, he packed some clothes and left. We didn't worry about it cause he's done that before, he would pack, walk out the front door and go around to the back patio, an hour or two, later he would come in." "Has he come in this time?" Mr. Norton asked. "No not yet." Frank replied. "Eileen went out, walked around the house, he's not here, I thought he was hiding and when it starting raining he would come in. I have been expecting him to walk in any moment." "Frank, you better call the police and tell them what you told me, the sooner you tell them the better their chances are of finding him."

Frank hung up the phone, he told Eileen that Mr. Norton has the medallion back, he told her the story of Mr. Short and that Jimmy was telling them the truth. "Oh no," she said "We have to call the police and tell them that Jimmy is missing." "No" Frank said, "We're going to the police station and tell them, get Jodie and make sure she is warm. I'll start the car." At the police station, the three of them went in, at the front desk Frank told the officer that his son was missing, then, proceeded to tell her the story about the missing medallion. He was talking fast hoping they would form a search party sooner. "Whoaaaa there, my name is officer, Kate Olson, you said your son is missing, how long has he been missing?" "He left home at 4:45 this afternoon." Frank told her. "We need some information, fill this out and return it to me, It will only take you a few minutes."

13

Frank sat next to Eileen, he started filling out the form it was a missing persons report. The information to be filled out on the form was their names, address, phone number, name of the missing person, his or her age. Their place of employment, the work phone number etc. When he was finished he took it back to Officer Olson, she read it, then told Mr. Shannon that it would be at least 72 hours before they can do anything, that his son might show up during that time, if not they would form a search party and start looking for him. That she would pass the information sheet along to the detectives, they would be in touch and handle it from there. Frank didn't believe that, "72 HOURS," he yelled, "My son could be anywhere, or he could be dead by that time, I'm going to form my own search party, and see if I can get my friends to help us look for him." That's up to you Mr. Shannon, I'm sure the detectives will be in touch." "Thanks for your help." Frank said in discuss.

Leaving the police station, Frank, Eileen and Jodie hurried to the car. It was the third of July, twilight is usually between eight and nine, by nine pm it is fully dark, right now, it is only seven pm it should still be daylight, with the clouds being almost totally black with just a few edges of white or a light grey covering the sky made it seem like night, the rain coming down and putting moisture in the air turned the night chilly, with the wind blowing at twenty to twenty five miles an hour ahead of the storm and sometimes gusting thirty five to forty five miles an hour made the chilly air down right cold.

Inside the car, Frank started the motor and turned on the heater, looking over at his wife, Frank asked, "Eileen . . . would you like to drive around town? . . . we could look for Jimmy, . . . with it raining, he could be standing under a store awning, or some kind of cover, it won't hurt to look, . . . what do you think?" Jodie spoke up, "I want to look for Jimmy. We could see him walking somewhere and bring him home." "Okay Frank," Eileen said, "it won't hurt to look, but what if we don't see him? What, then?" "It won't take long to cover the town, if we don't see him, we'll go home and I'll ask Jack to go with me, we can stop and ask people if they saw him, check the stores that are open, I'll need a picture of Jimmy."

They spent the next hour driving all over town, even alley ways, they never saw Jimmy. "Frank," Eileen said, "I would like to go home, I'll call Jimmy's friends. Maybe he went to one of their houses. You and Jack can look if you want." Frank went around the block and headed home, just then a bright flash of lightning ripped thru the sky and the thunder cracked and boomed like cannons being fired, then rumbled off in the distance. The rain poured down, Jodie, sitting in the back seat screamed, she started crying and shaking, "I . . . I want Jim . . . Jimmy, why won't he come home?" "It's, okay sweetheart," Eileen said, "The lightning and thunder are gone, we'll be home soon." "I want Jimmy," Jodie said, still crying, "Daddy, please find Jimmy."

When they arrived home, Frank parked the car in the garage, Eileen helped Jodie out. Entering the house Jodie literally ran thru the kitchen and up the stairs to her room. Eileen followed telling her not to run. In her room, she tried to settle her down, Jodie was still sniffling. "It's alright now, were in the house," Eileen was saying, "The lightning and thunder won't hurt us, let's get you ready for bed. Her mother helped her undress and put on her night gown, "Would you like a snack?" Eileen asked. "NO, I want Jimmy!" "You know Jimmy isn't here, your father is going to look for him."

Jodie got in bed and covered up, she then reached for the stuffed horse Jimmy had given her, it comforted her, made her feel at ease, it was something her big brother gave her with love. Her mother sat on the edge of the bed. Then Jodie said, "Mommy, I want Jimmy, he would still be here if you and daddy believed him, he didn't take a gold coin, he told me he didn't, Jimmy doesn't lie, and you didn't have to slap him, why are you and daddy mean to us? Right now . . . , I don't like you and daddy very much."

Eileen didn't know what to say about that, so she got up, said goodnight, she kissed Jodie on the cheek and left the room. On her way down stairs she thought about what Jodie had said. 'Why are you and daddy mean to us, right now I don't like you and daddy very much.' Eileen went to the kitchen she was still thinking about that while she made coffee. Seated at the table, Frank was on the phone talking to the next door neighbor, Mr. Jack Savage.

Chapter Three

Jimmy knew it was raining when he was in his room packing, before leaving his room he had put on his rain coat , when his father checked his backpack and all the pockets, he had also checked the pockets of Jimmy's rain coat. Standing on the front porch, he pulled the hood up over his head, and zipped up the front, he jiggled up and down a few times to settle the backpack then left the porch. "Dad Mom, why didn't you believe me, you called me a liar and a thief, you even slapped me when I said I didn't take that stupid gold coin, and when I said 'I won't stay where I'm not wanted,' why didn't you say 'You are wanted, and we love you. We don't want you to go.' but you didn't say anything like that when I left, so I will leave this town and never return, also I will never talk to either of you again," he said to himself quietly out loud as he left the yard and started walking down the street.

Even though it was only four forty five in the afternoon, it was still a little dark from the cloud cover and rain, Jimmy didn't hurry, he was hoping his parents would come after him, but they didn't. Now I know they don't want me, He said to himself. He walked into town and then he headed west, he decided to go into the mountains, that way he knew no one would be able to find him. When he was going thru town he was watching the people, no one seemed to pay attention to him, they, all were hurrying trying to get out of the rain. The cars in town were going slow with their head lights on and the wipers going. The hood over Jimmy's head covered his whole head except just a little of his face.

Reaching the west side of town, he was walking on the right side of the road, the rain had slowed to a sprinkle, he knew he had to get up into those mountains before dark and find a place to stay, to keep out of the weather, and for protection. He knew this from a few books he had read, and from animal planet, the history channel, and the weather channel on TV, as he was walking, he did notice a dirt road that seemed to go up into the mountains, or at least headed that way. He looked both ways there were no cars coming that was close, he did see some headlights a long way off, coming both ways so he ran across the road up to the fence that was parallel to the highway.

As the cars got closer, Jimmy knelt down so no one would see him, just in case his family was looking for him and they were asking questions to the people they talked to. He had made up his mind, his parents didn't want him or they would have never let him go. When the cars had passed he got up, made his way thru the fence and started walking toward the mountains, Jimmy was intelligent for a boy of ten, his mother would read to him and Jodie from time to time, and when they asked questions, she would answer them, or try to the best she could. Jodie, being only a seven year old, along with Jimmy had a great vocabulary. Jimmy liked to read, when he found a book that caught his attention he read it sometimes he would sit with Jodie and read to her.

Jimmy and Jodie loved animals, especially dogs they once asked their parents if they could have a dog, the answer was absolutely not. Another thing they liked to do together was watch animal planet on television, along with other learning programs that taught them how to do different things, such as all kinds of survival programs, hunting, fishing, how to survive in the wild, and how to make a snare to catch a rabbit or other kinds of animals for food.

Jimmy was following the dirt road south, actually it was just two ruts paralleling each other with grass and weeds growing in the middle, the road wasn't used much and there was grass and weeds growing in each rut in places, the road itself didn't go anywhere, or to any ones ranch, or farm. It just dead ended at the tree line. It was mainly used during hunting season. Jimmy walked in the middle thru the grass and weeds so he wouldn't leave his foot prints for others to follow.

When he reached the tree line, he stepped over the path on his right and started working his way up the mountain thru the trees, he kept climbing, using the trees and bushes to help pull himself upward, a few times one foot or the other would slip on the wet pine needles, every so often he would stop to rest, while resting he would look around to see if he could find some cover, some place to use as a shelter for he knew it would probably rain hard again between now and tomorrow morning.

During this rest period he realized he hadn't brought any food or water with him, 'Oh no.' he thought 'I'm going to be hungry soon, and real hungry in the morning, I'm already thirsty,' when he left the house he wasn't thinking about food or water, his thoughts were on leaving and what his mom and dad had said and the fact that his mom had slapped him in anger, and hard, he could still feel the slap on his left cheek, using his left hand he rubbed his face. "Calm down" he said to himself, "I have to figure things out, first things first, and right now I have to find some shelter."

He got up and started climbing again, it was slow going, an hour later he could see the top, he was having to work his way around, and under some huge granite boulders some stacked on top of each other, when he was on top, it was starting to get darker, he stood and looked toward town, he could see the street lights and some lights inside some of the business and homes.

'Homes.' he thought, 'I wish I was home now, but that isn't the fact, the fact is I am here. I am on my own and I have to use my wits. I have to think things out real careful. First I will find a place to spend the night. In the morning I will figure out what I have to do, remember Jimmy, first things first.' he looked to his left and saw part of the dirt road he used to get here, so he knew which way he had to go to keep going south, turning, he climbed down and made his way along the top of the ridge, just when it was dark enough where he could hardly see, he found a small cave among some rocks. Inside the cave was darker than outside, he made his way in by feeling his way and moving slow, he had to climb over some rocks, in what seemed like hours, but was actually a few minutes, he found a flat surface, and sat down. Using his hands he felt around very slowly, and he listened hard, hoping not to hear any sound that wasn't friendly. Satisfied, all was well, he relaxed, taking the backpack off he unbuckled the straps, took out his winter coat, he removed the rain coat and put on the winter coat.

He spread out the rain coat to use as a protective blanket in case the rain water came in, he wouldn't get to wet. He was tired, not sleepy, just tired. The next thing he knew, he was awaken by a loud boom and crackling noise, he sat up quickly, looking all around but it was pitch black, no matter which way he looked, so he sat still and listened, the lightning flashed across the sky again and Jimmy said 'one' when the thunder boomed and crackled rumbling through the clouds and over the mountains, rain came down hard, the wind was blowing hard enough to push the rain almost sideways. 'Wow.' Jimmy thought 'It sure does rain harder up here on the mountain.'

Since Jimmy was awake, he sat there staring into the darkness waiting for the next thunder and lightning, when it came, it was louder than ever, the thunder seemed to shake the ground, and the lightning was so bright he had to close his eyes, the thunder had rumbled away and all was quiet except the pouring rain, it was then Jimmy heard a whimpering sound, like a puppy, the pitch was high, he looked around again but couldn't see anything, sitting very still he heard it again, since he was facing the entrance to the cave, the sound of the puppy came from behind him, 'Oh no,' he thought 'That can't be a dog, not way up here, that has to be a wolf. It sounds like a puppy, I wonder if the mother wolf is in this cave too.' he felt for his backpack, opening the straps he felt around for his pocket knife, finding it, he closed the straps, opened one of the blades, then he turned around and yelled.

Hey, he shouted, then listened, no sound, he waited, there was no noise except the pounding of the rain, and his own heart, still facing the way the sound of the puppy came from, he laid down, next thing he knew it was morning, it was daylight but the sun still wasn't shinning, it was cloudy and still raining, there was no thunder and lightning, the storm had passed, only light showers, and sometime it just sprinkled. Now that he could see, he sat up and looked toward the back of the cave, he didn't believe his eyes, "Well I'll be" he said, "A baby wolf, you can't be more than a month old, where's your momma?"

On hands and knees he crawled his way toward the baby wolf, the wolf made a little growling noise, still watching Jimmy he backed up to the back wall, growling with a little whine, Jimmy stopped, "It's okay boy, I'm not going to hurt you!" sitting down, Jimmy held out one hand coaxing the wolf to come to him. It took a little time but wolf finally came to him in a playful mood, Jimmy picked him up and petted him, Jimmy looked around, he didn't see any other baby's, or the mother. "You don't have any brothers or sisters, your momma's not here, your, all alone just like me.

Carrying the wolf back to his backpack, he put the wolf down, he took off the winter coat and put it back in his pack, putting on the rain coat, he, put his pack on, picked up the wolf and left the cave. Out in the open he looked around, the sky was covered with clouds all grey and black, he couldn't see the town, the clouds were hanging low, creating a fog, but he did see the tops of the taller mountains where the tops were above the clouds, the fog had settled in the valleys winding around the mountains.

Two of them off to the east had what he called a funny shape, seeing the tops of those mountains he knew which way was south, he looked at the wolf, the wolf was all black with one white and one brown spot on the back of his head. "I'm going to call you 'BEAR'" he said. "When you grow up, you will remind me of a bear. There's those funny looking mountains over there bear, so south is this way" Carrying bear, Jimmy put him under his rain coat to keep him dry and warm, he started making his way south, he hadn't gone more than half a mile when he smelled a terrible odor, looking around trying to find the source, making his way around trees and bushes, twenty minutes later he found the source.

It was a dead wolf, the same color as bear all black, with a white and brown spot behind her head, the dead wolf had been torn apart and partly eaten. Even so, Jimmy could tell the wolf was a female, probably bears mother, Jimmy didn't stay there long, he headed south carrying bear, he didn't let bear see the dead wolf, the wind was blowing from the southwest so it carried the odor away from them, "Bear," he said "We have to find something to eat."

He had thought about cutting off some of the wolf meat, but then he thought better of it, "It probably doesn't taste good, and no telling how long it's been dead." He said to himself. Going along the top of the mountain, he came to the highest point, climbing up some rocks he sat and looked all around, holding bear on his lap and petting him he said, "Look bear, all these beautiful mountains, the different colors of green, the clouds low in the valleys creating a fog, the higher clouds dark and threatening rain, hiding the sun. These mountains are so beautiful, one of GOD's greatest creations! Well bear, it's time to go, we have to find something to eat." Securing bear in his rain coat, he climbed down and headed south.

All day, he worked his way down one mountain side and up another and down again, winding his way around foot hills, across valleys and clearings. Every time he came to a spring, creek or small river, if the water was clear, he and bear would drink, several times when he came to a spring or creek the water was dirty and muddy, he would cross it and keep going. In the valleys and clearings the tall weeds and grass was still wet from all the rain, the sun hidden behind the clouds couldn't shine upon the earth, the sun rays didn't penetrate the clouds to warm the earth and dry the valleys and clearings. Carrying bear, Jimmy walked through the tall weeds and grass, across the valleys and clearings, his pants was wet up to and above his knees.

Jimmy and bear wasn't thirsty, they were hungry, walking through a valley, Jimmy was thinking, I left home yesterday, Saturday, so today is Sunday. I haven't eaten since noon yesterday when I went with my dad to his work, that's when all the trouble started. No wonder I'm hungry, sorry bear, I will try to find us both something to eat.' Then he said to bear, "I know we can live awhile without food, but not without water, I know this from a survival show I saw on TV, but I don't think we have to worry about that, there are creeks and small rivers in these mountains.'

Chapter Four

Frank went straight to the phone he started to call his neighbors to see if they would help look for Jimmy. The first one he called was his next door neighbor on the right, Jack and Kathleen Savage, they had two daughters, Pauline, and Julie, Pauline was twelve and Julie was nine. When Frank called, Jack answered, "Hello" "Jack, this is Frank, sorry to bother you, but Jimmy is missing, I'm asking you for your help, I am going to organize a search party to look for him, his mother and I are very worried, can I count on you?" "Yes, of course you can Frank," Jack replied, "But how, when did this happen?"

"It was this afternoon, his mother and I was questioning him about something that happened earlier today, we were mad, Jimmy was mad he said he was leaving home, he said he didn't want to stay where he wasn't wanted, you know he has done this before, walked out the front door, went around to the back, then a couple hours later he would come in." "yeah, I know, this time he didn't come in?" "No," Frank replied. "Frank, you have to call the police, and file a missing person report." "We just got home from the police station, I filled out a report, and told them what happened, they said there was nothing they could do for seventy two hours, that it is possible that Jimmy will return during that time, if not, they would organize a search party and start looking. I told them Jimmy could be anywhere by that time, or even dead. I want to start looking tonight."

"Frank, that's non sense, it's, dark, and it's raining, Jimmy, would have found some place to hide to get out of the rain. He won't be out in the open. There's nothing you can do tonight, you would just drive

22

around looking and see or find nothing, wait till morning and I will help you organize a search party, then we can all look, all over town, and even out in the country, if we find anything, then the police will have to get involved." "Jack, I just can't sit here and do nothing I feel like I am letting my family down, that I should be doing something, even if it's wrong."

"I know Frank, I would feel the same way, you are not thinking logically because it's Jimmy that's missing. I would feel that way if Pauline or Julie were missing." "Thanks Jack, I know you are just trying to be logic about this, but I have to try." "Alright Frank, give me ten minutes and I'll go with you, two pair of eyes are better than one, besides you have to watch the road, I can keep looking." "Thanks Jack, you are a true friend, come over when you're ready, I'll wait for you here." Jack told his wife Kathleen that Jimmy was missing, and Frank wanted him to help look for him tonight. He asked Kathleen to call some of the neighbors and let the know, and that we are going to form a search party in the morning, and ask them to call their neighbors and friends, were going to need as many people as we can get. Kathleen agreed.

Ten minutes later, Frank and Jack were in Frank's car heading toward the center of town, with headlights on and wipers pulsating, Frank turned on the flashers and slowed down, he went down one street and up the other, "See anything yet Jack?" Frank asked. "No Frank, I don't, I see dark places with even darker shadows, not very many people out tonight, do you want to stop and ask questions? He could be holed up in one of the hotel or motel lobby's. It wouldn't hurt to ask. Do you have a picture of Jimmy? "Yeah, I have one. Eileen got one for me before you came over." "Okay, there's a motel coming up, let's start there. By the way, I asked Kathleen to call some neighbors, to let them know about the search party, and to ask them to pass the word, we will need all the help we can get, the bigger the search party the better. We will know in the morning." "Thanks," Frank said.

They pulled into a motel, parked under the overhead cover in front of the lobby both men got out and went in. At the registration desk, Jack said, "Good evening Miss, did you happen to see a boy about ten years old this evening, by himself?" "No, I can't say that I have, I've seen young boys about that age with their parent's, but not by himself. Are you the police?" "No ma'am," said Frank, "I'm the boy's father, reaching, underneath his jacket, he pulled the picture out of his shirt pocket, he showed it to her, "His name is James Lee Shannon, Jimmy for short, he's been missing since around four forty-five this afternoon." "I'm so sorry Mr. Shannon," she said, looking at the picture. "If I had seen this little boy, I would remember, he sure is a handsome young man."

"Thank you ma-am your very kind." Have you been on duty long?" "Miss Jackson, Silvia Jackson, I've been on duty since four this afternoon." Miss Jackson was an average looking woman, thirty four with long auburn hair, green eyes, her height, five foot four inches, weight is one hundred eighteen, very little make-up, she had on dark blue slacks, white blouse with a bow tied at the neck, and a light blue jacket. Her appearance and manner was professional. "I'm sorry," she said again, "I wish I could help you." "Thank you, Miss Jackson," Jack said, "If you see him, will you give us a call?" He handed her a piece of paper with Frank's phone number. "Yes of course, I get off at midnight, it's now 8:30, I will call if I see him before my shift ends." Frank asked her to pass the information on to the person who relieves her, and to call him if Jimmy is seen, no matter the time.

They left the motel heading west, the rain had slowed to a soft sprinkle, driving slow, they both watched both sides of the road to no avail, the traffic was nonexistent, with flashers on and wipers pulsating, Frank drove for five miles, "Jimmy couldn't have come this far, could he?" Frank asked. "Well, it is 9:15, that's four and a half hours, if Jimmy kept walking, he could be this far. Do you want to go a bit farther, just to make sure?" jack said, "There is one more possibility, he knows your car, if he saw us at the motel he might be hiding, you did say he was upset when he left." "You don't mind if we look around some more?" Frank asked, "He still could be hiding in town somewhere." "Alright Frank, let's keep looking for another hour or so, if we don't see him during that time, we have to figure he found a place to spend the night. Tomorrow, during daylight hours with a search party we can cover more ground in all directions."

For the next two hours, while in town they stopped at several hotels and motels, the desk clerks all said the same thing. They had not seen a little boy ten years old or any age alone. Outside the rain came down harder, the lightning flashed brightly and the thunder boomed and crackled across the sky. Leaving the last hotel they checked they went up and down every street, criss-crossing every intersection and side street. They even went thru every alley in town, some times in the alley they would stop and check in the dumpsters, when there was a dumpster. It was now eleven twenty pm, there search was fruitless so they decided to call it quits till morning. Arriving at the house, Frank and Jack said good-night, inside the house Eileen was waiting, when Frank told her what they did and who they talked to, that they didn't find or see hide or hair of Jimmy, Eileen broke down, she started crying. Frank held her he tried to console her but it didn't work.

Jodie was upstairs in her room sleeping, Eileen sat down at the table still crying, Frank, got her a glass of water and himself a cup of hot coffee, putting the cup on the table he sat down. "Eileen," he said, "We did what we could, being it's a rainy night. Tomorrow, with a search party, and daylight, we will be able to cover ten times the area that Jack and I did tonight, there was no more we could do." "I know Frank," she said, "It's just that I keep thinking of Jimmy out there all alone in this bad weather, and I keep thinking how he told us he didn't take that stupid medallion," Raising her voice, "WE DIDN'T BELIEVE HIM, I even slapped him, Frank, do you know how that makes me feel, do you think we will find him?" "Yes Eileen, I do, but right now, I think we should go to bed, we have to get up early so we can get started at first light, we, have a long day ahead of us." Eileen took a long drink of water.

"If we do find him, do you think he will forgive us? Forgive me for slapping him!" she asked. "Yes I do," he answered, "Kids are very forgiving they are young and depend on their parents for everything. Kids always believe what their parents tell them to be the truth. Why did you ask that?"

"If Jimmy and Jodie believe what we tell them to be the truth, why didn't we believe Jimmy, and why are we so mean and strict with them? We should be more tolerant and understanding, if we were, Jimmy wouldn't have left, and he wouldn't have gotten upset and sat on the patio all those times." "Eileen, what brought all this on, you know I miss Jimmy as much as you do, and I'm just as worried. Tomorrow, there will be a lot of us looking for him one of us might find him." "What if we don't find him, not ever, he'll be out of our lives forever we will never know what happened to him, I could never forgive myself." "Eileen . . . I don't know what to say to that."

At that moment Frank knew what Eileen was trying to say. "When we find Jimmy," he was saying, "We can bring him home, if you want, we can sit him down and tell him how sorry we are, we can ask him to forgive us, and let him and Jodie know we will be better parents."

"You promise Frank, really promise to be a better parent, I know I can, we could be a much happier family!" she said with tears in her eyes. "I promise Eileen, I really promise you and I will be a better parent. They turned out the lights, Frank made sure all the doors were locked, they went upstairs and retired for the night, lying in bed Eileen whispered. "Dear LORD, please take good care of Jimmy, keep him safe during this night, give us the strength to get through this and the strength to find him. You gave him to us, please don't take him away." Then she went to sleep.

Chapter Five

Jimmy was carrying bear, and making their way south, he topped a small rise, looking around and seeing only taller mountains in all directions, he looked straight ahead to the south only to see more mountains, "Well bear," he said, "It looks like there are only mountains all around, I know you are hungry, so am I." He took a few steps, watching where he was going the mountain side started slopping downhill he stopped. "Look bear, down there." He was looking over the tree tops at lower elevation, "It's a small clearing with a stream of water, let's go down there, we can get a drink and there might be something to eat." He worked his way down the hill side he slipped a few times and slid a few feet each time. The clearing was bigger than it looked from the top of the mountain, and the stream was wider than just a small creek.

Putting bear down, Jimmy started looking around for food, any kind of food, wild vegetables, a wounded animal, anything, he was that hungry and he knew bear was. He knew from watching TV that wild vegetables grew along the edge of rivers and creeks. He went to the edge of the small river, knelt down, cupped his hand, scooping up some water, he drank.

The small river was ice cold and running clear and it taste good, he looked around for bear, bear was over by some bushes smelling some grass and weeds, picking bear up he went back to the river cupped his hand, scooping up some more water, he put his hand by bears nose, bear touched the water with his nose then started drinking, he drank all the water in Jimmy's hand so he scooped up some more for him, bear drank all the water again. "Thirsty bear," said Jimmy, "Well you can have all

27

you want." he scooped more water and bear drank almost all of it. He then started searching the edge of the water along the bank. He found a few wild something, he wasn't sure what they were, dipping them into the running water he rinsed the dirt off then he took a small bite out of one, "Hmmmm," he said," this tastes like a turnip." He remembered that from when his mother cooked them, 'It's not bad raw' he thought, when he tasted the other one, it was an onion.

Jimmy didn't like onions, but he was hungry enough it didn't matter he was going to eat it. He knew this would help with his hunger but what about bear, he knew he had to get some milk or meat, somewhere, He wasn't going to let bear die. After checking both sides of the river thru the clearing, from tree line to tree line, he only found a few more wild vegetables, after he picked up bear, he stood there looking about the clearing, it wasn't a small clearing it was a huge valley, with mountains all around. From the top of the mountain where he first saw it, most of the valley was obscured by the pine trees. "Well bear," he said," let's see if we can find you something to eat." When he crossed the river which came up to his knees, he continued moving south. By midafternoon, he had crossed the valley and was walking along the side of another smaller mountain, again going around trees and bushes, working his way down, he was close to the bottom where the ground leveled out some and the going would be easier, it was then that he heard what he thought was a car horn.

Hearing this, he didn't believe it he was in the mountains 'There are no roads up here in these mountains' he thought. He stopped anyway and sat down behind a pine tree, he watched and listened, soon he heard it again, he, then thought he heard the roar of an engine. Looking in the direction from which he heard the engine, he soon saw a jeep coming out of the trees on the other side of the clearing, from where he was and where the jeep was, he guessed it to be the length of two football fields. Sitting there and watching, the jeep was heading straight for him, then all of a sudden it stopped, he saw a man and a woman come out of the jeep, they disappeared around the back, a minute later, when he saw them again, they were carrying something, they walked toward him a ways then stopped, spreading a blanket and putting down a basket. Jimmy said to bear, quietly, "Their on a picnic bear, let's watch to see what they do, we don't want them to see us."

While he was watching them, he realized that they were young, in their twenties maybe. The young man and woman went running off, they were headed toward him then veered off to Jimmy's left. He sat motionless and watched them till they disappeared into the edge of the trees. He couldn't see them, but he could hear them, sitting very still and quiet, he listened, even though they were not anywhere near him, he soon heard some laughter and some moaning, it didn't sound like someone was hurt, it was a different moan. It was like a moan of excitement, he figured they were busy and happy at whatever they were doing.

He made his way down the rest of the hill and started across the clearing to where the picnic basket was, he kept looking back to make sure they had not seen him, when he reached the blanket, he looked all around, not seeing anyone else or any animal he laid down. Once on the ground, he faced the way the man and woman went, he went thru the basket. He saw a small square carrying case, opening it he saw two bottles of tea and two cartons of milk, some sandwiches, fruit, cupcakes, and other things in the basket at the bottom he saw a hunting knife in its sheath. He thought long and hard while lying there, he knew the basket wasn't his, and he was not a thief, but he and bear was starving, I have no choice, he decided.

He looked around, he could not see the man and woman, he grabbed the basket by the handle, pulling it off the blanket, then he pulled on the blanket, putting it in the basket, when he was done, he crawled backward, he made his way to the rear of the jeep, then he stood up, looking thru the windows, he still didn't see them, so keeping the jeep between him and them, holding bear in his right arm under his rain coat and the basket in his left hand, he backed away, walking backward he made his way into the trees from the direction which they had come.

Once in the trees where he knew they couldn't see him, he headed south again, not running, but walking at a fast pace. He wanted to make as less noise as possible, well away from the jeep he started running. He was still running when he heard someone yell . . . , "NOOO . . . ," hearing that, he knew the man and woman had come back to the jeep and found the blanket and basket gone. He hoped they would think a bear or some kind of animal took them, being in the forest among the trees, he was running on fallen pine needles, he knew there were no foot prints or sound for them to follow so they wouldn't be coming after him.

Still heading south, Jimmy stopped running, he was breathing hard so he stopped to rest a few minutes and to catch his breath. "Bear," he said "I have food for us. We can't stop now, we'll go a little farther then we'll stop and I'll feed you." Starting out again, Jimmy made his way toward the top of the nearest hill, 'Maybe I can find us a place to stay the night,' he thought, walking and thinking about what he had done, he told himself, 'I am not a liar or a thief, bear and I are starving that's why I took it', he saw some rocks and boulders, he made his way to them, all the while looking for some place to stay, he didn't find one, so he went on, making his way down the other side, he saw what he thought was a hole in the ground, going over to it, he saw that it was like a cave in the ground or a wolf den.

He could see the back of it, so he knew it wasn't very big or deep, but it should be dry and keep the wind and cold rain off them, should it rain, and the way it looks it will rain any minute. It has been cloudy all day but the rain held off. Entering the small hole, he smelled a strange odor, one he couldn't identify. Jimmy put bear and the basket down, took off his raincoat and spread it out, inside up. The air being damp and chilly, he got his winter coat out and put it on.

He was glad the raincoat was clear plastic and not yellow like his sister Jodie's, if it was, the man and woman might have seen him. Jimmy sat on the raincoat, going thru the basket he also found two plastic cups, four bottles of water, taking out one of the cups and the milk, he, poured the milk into the cup. "Bear, I have some food for you." reaching for bear, Jimmy held him in his right arm, placing the half filed cup at bear's nose like he did the water, bear smelled the cold milk then started lapping it up. "Good boy," Jimmy said, "I knew you were hungry, and since you are just a little guy, and I don't know when you ate last, this is all you can have for now, I'll give you some more later." After bear drank all the milk, Jimmy put him down and got a sandwich for himself, he pulled out ham and cheese, while eating, Jimmy, pulled a small piece of ham off and gave it to bear.

After he ate the sandwich, he opened one of bottles of water, took a drink, reaching in the basket he took out the hunting knife, taking the knife out of the sheath, he inspected it, it was a ten inch bowie knife and it was sharp with a very sharp point. He looked outside and noticed it was getting dark 'Be raining soon,' he thought, sitting there looking out, he thought of home, his mom, dad and Jodie, he missed them all especially Jodie, but because of what had happened and what his folks accused him of, remembering the slap, he knew he could never go home. He missed Jodie and he missed watching TV, then he remembered what he saw about surviving in the wilderness, on one of those survival programs. When finding a place to spend the night, always secure your surroundings the best you can, thinking of this, he decided to cut some branches to cover the entrance, to make it harder for any other animal to get in, and hoping that the animal with that strange odor doesn't come back and want in.

It started raining when he was cutting the branches, not hard at first, and he knew it would soon, he tried to hurry, chopping enough branches, he dragged them to the cave, backing in he pulled the branches in and arranged them so they were as sturdy as he could make them, hoping that no wild animal would try to get in during the night, also that bear couldn't get out. Before night fall, it did rain harder, like the night before on top of the mountain, the lightning flashed brightly and the thunder boomed it seemed to be louder than last night because it was echoing off the side of the mountain. Looking through the branches Jimmy saw a lightning flash, the lightning struck a small pine tree farther down the mountain from where he was, the pine tree caught on fire, and then the rain came down so hard Jimmy couldn't see more than five feet past the opening.

He kept looking through the branches, when the lightning flashed again he could see the burning tree from the glare of the fire, as the rain poured down, it extinguished the fire. Since he and bear wasn't going anywhere, he decided to give bear some more milk, filling the cup half full, and with bear standing in front of him, he placed the cup on the ground in front of bear, Smelling the milk, bear drank vigorously.

While bear was drinking his milk, Jimmy checked the opening to the cave to see if any water was coming in, there wasn't, the entrance was on a downhill slope toward the outside and what water dripped off the top either soaked in the ground or ran down hill away from the cave opening. Knowing they would be dry, Jimmy felt better. It was dark now so Jimmy put everything back in the basket, he then picked up bear and laid down, the air was a little chilly, he, covered them both with the blanket. With bear fed, and he himself feeling better after eating the wild vegetables and the sandwich, he felt content, bear being under the blanket nudged his way up to Jimmy arm and laid down, Jimmy petted him, with them both feeling content they went to sleep.

All through the night it rained, the lightning struck out, cutting horizontally through the sky and the thunder boomed and crackled as the stormed passed over. Jimmy would just get sleep when the thunder boomed, it would wake him up every time, he would sit up quickly and look around, looking out the opening, he looked for any kind of movement, but it pitch black. Listening hard for any sound, he heard nothing but the rain hitting the ground and the wind whistling through the trees, 'This place and these mountains sure are scary.' he thought. Laying down and checked on bear, making sure he was alright, sometimes bear would wake up, when he did, he would raise his head point his ears forward as if he heard something. Each time bear did this, Jimmy would sit up, he paid close attention to what bear was trying to tell him, that something was out there.

Maybe a bear, could it be a mountain lion or wolf, maybe even a pack of wolves he didn't know, there were no lights, nothing not even the moon could be seen to shine its light on the mountain side. Jimmy listened long and hard, same as he did last night, at the same time he watched bear, he wanted to see what his reaction would be if he did hear something. When bear settled down, Jimmy felt relieved, but he kept a close eye all around, as much as he could see. The rain was starting to ease up and Jimmy could see a little farther, it didn't help much, but more important, he didn't hear anything either.

While the storm was passing over head, Jimmy would just barely be asleep, then wake up, asleep, wake up each time the storm released its energy. By early morning before daylight the storm had moved east and the thunder that woke him up was less frequent and not as loud, Jimmy was finally able to get some sleep.

Chapter Six

When the alarm went off at five am, it woke Frank and Eileen up, Frank reached over to turn it off, they, laid there for a few minutes trying to wake up. It was the next day, the fourth of July, Eileen was thinking this when she realized it was Jimmy's birthday, "Frank, today is Jimmy's birthday," she said, "and he's not here." "I know Eileen, I was thinking the same thing we better get up and get things ready for the search party." "I'm going to take a shower," she responded, "you check on Jodie, while you are in the shower I'll fix breakfast." "Do you want me to wake her up, and get her bath ready?" He asked.

Thinking Eileen said, "No, let her sleep, we'll have time for that later after we eat, I'll get her up and give her a bath while you do the dishes, then I will fix her breakfast." The dawn was breaking when Eileen and Jodie came down stairs she asked Jodie what she wanted for breakfast. "Just toast" Jodie replied. Eileen started preparing it. Sitting at the table drinking coffee, Frank looked out the window, he didn't see any cars. "I better call Jack to see if Kathleen was able to get any of the neighbors to help us." While he was saying this the phone rang.

"Frank, I knew you would be up." "Morning Jack, I was going to call you, how did Kathleen make out on getting some of the neighbors to help?" "When we got home last night, she told me she got hold of Susan Merrill, Molly Perkins, and Jane Langly, they all agreed to help, Kathleen said they would tell their husbands, also call some more neighbors and friends, so I really don't know how many will show up. They were told to be here at seven thirty this morning."

At seven thirty Frank, Eileen and Jodie went outside, they looked up and down the street, no moving cars in sight, then Jack, Kathleen, Pauline and Julie came out, greeting each other, Jack said, "Don't worry Eileen, we will do our best to find Jimmy." "I know Jack," she said "I want to help look, I can be with Frank." "But who will take care of Jodie?" Jack asked. "I will," said Kathleen, "I can understand Eileen wanting to help look, Jimmy's her son, if no one minds, I will stay here and take care of the kids. Besides someone has to stay here in case Jimmy comes home or anyone needs me to make phone calls, or go on errands." "That's a good idea, at least we won't have to worry about the kids." said Frank.

While Frank was talking, a car horn sounded, they all turned toward the street, looking both ways, they saw a line of twenty cars coming from their left and fifteen cars coming from the right, every car was filled with men and women, at least five in each car. They stopped along the street bumper to bumper and everyone got out and walked up to where the others were, "Here we are," said Molly "Kathleen said you need our help to find Jimmy, what can you tell us?" Frank Said, "Before I explain, I would first like to say to all of you, on behalf of Eileen, Jodie and myself, Thank you so very much for being here, we certainly do need your help."

The others were listening while Frank explained, he told them about yesterday and about his conversations with Mr. Norton, he emphasized the fact that Jimmy did not take the gold medallion, he also mentioned how in the past, a few times Jimmy would seem to be upset, walk out the front door and go around back to the patio, then come in a little later, and that's what he and Eileen figured he would do this time, but he didn't. He told them what he and Jack did last night. "Frank, you don't have to explain to us, just tell us what you want us to do." said Mr. Perkins.

While Frank was talking, he also counted heads. "Thank you Mr. Perkins. There are one hundred seven nine of us here, I would like us to split up, we can go into the middle of town, and make four groups, each group will cover in different directions, North, East, South and West. If the police ask any questions, tell them you are looking for Jimmy Shannon, that he is missing, and that I filed a missing person report last night." "That's about it, is everyone ready to start looking?" asked Jack. "YEAH," they all shouted. "One more thing," Jack said, "Kathleen is going to stay here and watch the kids, make sure there is at least one person in each group with a cell phone, If we need to make any calls, call Kathleen and tell her what you need or want, and she can handle it from there, the reason being, we may have some dead spots during the search and won't be able to get through on a cell, Kathleen can use the land line, okay ladies and gentlemen, let's go and get this search underway.

Everyone got back into the cars they came in Jack went with Frank and Eileen. When everyone was in town and parked, they all met at the town square, someone had suggested that each group should have a hand held two way walkie-talkie in case someone finds something, they can let the others know. Frank said he thought it was a good idea, he asked the others to start searching and he would wait for radio shack to open and buy four good radios, the type that had a long range, and he would make sure each group had one. It was also mentioned that it might rain. With the black sky and lightning flashing and thunder rumbling off in the distance, everyone knew it would rain sometime today. Mr. Perkins and fourteen others went east, Mr. Merrill with his group went south, Mr. Langly and group went north the rest went west. Eileen went with Jack she knew her husband would catch up after he distributed the radios.

All four search parties was checking everywhere and everything in all four directions, each group had a picture of Jimmy, the one with the picture would go into whatever business was open and ask everyone there if they had seen him, each response was the same no, they also asked the store owner or manager if they could put up a poster in the window when they are printed, and leave it up till the boy is found.

When the owner or manager started Hee-Hawing, he or she was informed that Jimmy was born right there in Billings, that he was one of them, they were granted permission. Radio shack opened at nine thirty, he told the clerk that he wanted four two-way radios, all on the same channel, and ones that could reach out a long distance, The clerk informed him that two-way radios only reached out about a mile if there was no interference, what he needed was hand held CB radios, they have two or three channels and can reach out a good five miles if conditions were right.

Buying four CB radios and batteries, along with extra batteries, he and the clerk made sure all four radios were working, the clerk showed him how to install the battery, it took one square nine volt battery, the clerk also informed him that the battery will last a long time with intermitting use, so Frank knew it was a good idea to buy sixteen extra batteries, four for each radio, hoping they would find Jimmy and not need the radios or batteries after today.

In his car he went to each group and gave one of the men a radio and four extra batteries, he said we all will be using channel one, he then headed west to catch up with Eileen. When he arrived, he parked behind a police unit with the red and blue lights flashing, walking up to Eileen who was talking to the officer, Frank identified himself, asking what's wrong, Eileen told him nothing is wrong, the officer is just checking their story about Jimmy being missing, and they filed a missing persons report, that they were at the police station last night, and told officer Kate Coletrain they were organizing their own search party, since the police won't do anything for seventy two hours.

Finishing up with dispatch officer Dale Suddeth went over to the group, he informed them that dispatch confirmed their story, that the missing person's report was turned over to Detective Sgt. James Collinsworth, he also informed Mr. and Mrs. Shannon that Sgt. Collinsworth would be in touch with them on Monday, to go over the report, and to see if Jimmy had returned home or not, he also informed them that Sgt. Collinsworth would go over police proceedure with them.

"I don't care about that," Frank told officer Suddeth, "We just want our son back home." "I know you do, Mr. Shannon, no more than we do, but right now our hands are tied, like I said Sgt. Collinsworth will contact you, I'm sure he will arrange a search party, if your son hasn't returned by then. "Today is Sunday," Frank said in a discusted tone, "so what you are saying is, Sgt. Collinsworth will contact us tomorrow morning sometime?" "Yes sir." "In the meantime we're not breaking any laws by searching ourselves, are we?" "No sir." "Fine, then we will continue searching. Thank you for your time and concern, officer Suddeth.

By the time officer Suddeth left and they started their search it was midmorning, the sky was darker and the storm was getting closer, the lightning flashed more frequently and brighter and the thunder boomed louder and crackled as it disappeared over the mountains. "We're in for a down pour!" said Jack, "Let's check with the other groups, see how they're doing," When Frank gave each group a radio he told them which group they were, group one was going north, group two east, group three south, and his group is group four. Frank raised the radio and pressed the talk button. "Groups one, two, and three this is group four, find anything yet?"

"No, Frank, not yet, we are at the edge of town, do you want us to continue?" said Mr. Langly. North group leader, all three other groups said the same thing, they had found nothing, and no one has seen an ten year old boy by himself, they were all at the edge of town on all sides, all four groups had spread out, covering every street, every alley, they talked to every person they met. They had circled the town. Frank was informed by all three groups that they searched everywhere, and everything a boy could hide in, every person they talked to had the same answer. Pushing the talk button Frank said, "No, the storm is almost here and from the looks of it were in for a real gully washer," It was 4:10 in the afternoon, the sky was black, the lightning flashed and the thunder boomed. "Let's call it quits for today," Frank told them, "tomorrow we can start searching the country side. Everybody head back your cars, before we all get wet."

By the time everyone was at their cars, it had started raining, slowly at first, then all of a sudden the lightning flashed in several places at the same time, striking the ground and cutting across the sky, the thunder boomed and cracked immediately rumbling across the mountains and the rain poured down, the lightning flashed more frequent, and the thunder boomed like cannons, everybody was in their vehicles heading home.

They all agreed to take time off from work and help in the search, when Frank, Eileen and Jack arrived home, Eileen went with Jack to get Jodie, they could hear the phone ringing so Frank hurried to answer it, by the time he unlocked the door, got to the phone it stopped ringing. He checked the answering machine, there were three messages, he pushed play they were from the newspaper in town. 'Mr. Shannon, this is Tom Boyle with the times, we heard your son is missing, we would like to help, call me so we can discuss how the newspaper can help, the number is,"

Mr. Boyle gave the number each time he called, Frank put on a pot of coffee, then started to get out the makings for dinner, they decided on sandwiches, something quick, he was setting the table when Eileen and Jodie came in, they were both soaked from the down pour, "Let Jodie and me change, then we'll eat." Eileen said as she headed straight for the stairs. After setting the table for dinner, Frank went to the phone and dialed the newspaper, he asked for Mr. Boyle. "Mr. Boyle speaking, how may I help you?" Mr. Boyle, this is Mr. Shannon, We just got home, I heard your messages and am returning your call I would like to discuss how the newspaper can help us find Jimmy. I'm open to suggestions, how can you help?"

"Well Mr. Shannon, we can help in a few ways you don't have access to, we can publish in the paper that your son Jimmy is missing and ask our readers to help in the search. There is also a team of about fifty men in Butte who are very good at searching these mountains for lost people they do it every summer also they have two helicopters. You know these mountain are rugged and sometimes people get stranded on the side of a cliff when they try to climb it . . . And sometimes they get lost, they can't find their way back, that's when the helicopter is used, the lost one are usually found in a clearing waving their arms, get picked up and brought back."

"Mr. Boyle, how much will it cost me to place the advertisement in your paper?" "It won't cost you anything Mr. Shannon," said Mr. Boyle, "The paper does this as a public service, but before we can print it, we have to have your permission." "You have my permission Mr. Boyle will it be in tomorrow's paper?" "Yes sir, it will, the press hasn't started yet, I still have time to get this notice to them . . . . and if you don't mind, I will call the rescue team and ask them to help." "No sir Mr. Boyle, I don't mind at all!" "Very well Mr. Shannon, I will take care of it." "Thank you Mr. Boyle, It's been a pleasure talking to you." Bye.

When Eileen and Jodie came down, they were both dry and had change clothes. The coffee was done and Frank had the table all set, he was pouring two cups of coffee, he got Jodie a small glass of juice. During dinner he told Eileen about the phone messages, that he called them and talked to Mr. Boyle, he told her about the conversation. "Do you think we will find Jimmy?" She asked. "I don't know I hope so." Raising her voice she said "YOU HOPE SO, FRANK HE'S OUR SON." Trying to stay calm he replied, "I know he's our son, I want him home as bad as you do, but let's be realistic about this, he could be anywhere he could have gone in any direction, we just don't know, all we can do is hope that he is found. With all of us searching in all directions our chances of finding him has improve, not much, but they have improved. And if the rescue team uses a helicopter, they can search a much wider area."

"I can't stand this!" Eileen said "The waiting, the not knowing." She got up from the table and ran upstairs, Frank left Jodie sitting in her chair and followed Eileen upstairs. In their bedroom she was lying on the bed crying. Frank went to her, helping her to sit up, he put his arms around her and held her close. "Go ahead and cry," he whispered, "Let it all out, it might help . . . sometimes . . . , I feel like crying." Frank held her for a long time, letting her cry. He didn't say anything more, he just held her, finally he said in a low voice, "I'll go clean up in the kitchen and take care of Jodie.

After the kitchen was cleaned up and everything put away, he and Jodie went into the front room, turned on the TV to the weather channel, the forecast for the next five days called for clearing skies, sun shine and a warm breeze five to ten miles an hour from the southwest, at nine pm Frank put Jodie to bed then went down stairs to make sure the doors were locked, he turned out all the lights except the front room. Frank sat all alone in his recliner looking at the TV, but he didn't see it, he didn't even know what was on, he was thinking about Jimmy. He sat there for a long time going over the past two days in his mind, wondering how could he have been so mean, why didn't he believe Jimmy, he was his son, he raised him, but most of all, how could he have been so cold hearted, to just let Jimmy walk out like that. It was then that he broke down and cried. After a while he went upstairs to bed, Eileen was already asleep, he turned out the light got in bed and closed his eyes.

It was a little after midnight Eileen was dreaming about Jimmy. She had dreamt that they found him at the top of the first mountain north of town. In her dream, she was with Frank and a few other members of the search team when they found him. But what they found was his body. Jimmy was lying between two trees face down, he had on his clear plastic rain coat, shirt, pants, and work shoes, everything looked fine, they thought he was sleeping, when they called his name, he didn't move. Frank went to him and he shook him calling his name, "Jimmy," still no movement. When Frank turned him over on his back, Eileen saw the front of him, Jimmy's face was half torn away, his clothes had been shredded, and he was bloody from head to toe, Jimmy was dead. She let out a blood curdling scream.

In her dream, when she screamed, it woke her up she sat up quickly crying Jimmy's name out loud. Screaming Jimmy's name also woke up Frank and Jodie. Frank sat up startled, Jodie started crying Frank comforted Eileen then went to Jodie's room to comfort her, holding her he said "Mommy had a dream, everything is okay!" He stayed with Jodie for a little while holding her, she calmed down and went back to sleep. Putting her in bed, he covered her up and left the room.

Back in his bedroom, Eileen was sitting on the edge of the bed, she was shaking like she was cold, but she wasn't, she was scared, frightened at the thought of her son being dead. Frank sat down beside her, he told her Jodie was okay, and that she was sleeping. He didn't say anything else he was waiting to see if she wanted to talk about her dream. She just sat there, not saying a word, finally Frank put his arm around her and said softly, "C'mon hon, try to get some sleep, they both got back in bed and covered up, Frank curled up next to her, he put his arm around her on the outside of the blanket, holding her they both drifted back to sleep.

Chapter Seven

Jimmy, lying in the small hole in the side of the mountain, or a small cave as he called it, was sound asleep with bear curled up next to him, he was awaken by a loud sound, startled he sat up and listened, looking through the brush he had put in front of the opening he saw nothing. It was still dark, Jimmy's sitting up suddenly woke up bear, he started whimpering so Jimmy picked him up and petted him to keep him quiet, "shhhh," he whispered then he heard the noise again, only this time he thought he knew what it was. In his mind he was thinking a big wolf or a big bear. Bear, (the wolf pup,) was content with Jimmy's petting and stopped whimpering, Jimmy put him down and reached for his backpack, opening it he got out the bowie knife and waited.

Sitting there waiting, watching and listening, he tried to tell himself he wasn't afraid, but deep down inside he knew he was, bear was by his side, holding the knife in his right hand he kept petting bear with his left to try to stay calm and to keep bear from whimpering, maybe the wolf or bear would go away. As he sat there listening, he heard something walking around then he heard a stick break, the sound was loud in the quiet morning and he knew whatever it was, was getting closer to the small opening. He was looking through the branch's at the entrance when he saw whatever it was walk past, as dark as it was he couldn't be sure. A shadow was all he saw, 'I'm safe as long as I stay in here and that thing whatever it is stay's out there.' he thought.

It seemed to take forever but dawn finally came, as it was getting lighter the sun was peeking over the mountains and the rain had stopped, now that Jimmy could see inside the small cave, he got the milk and a cup out of the basket, poured the cup half full of milk and fed bear, while bear was drinking the milk, he ate one of the ham and cheese sandwiches. Still listening for strange sounds and keeping an eye on the opening, he saw and heard nothing. After he and bear had eaten, with the knife in his hand he pushed the branches away from the entrance and went outside, he wanted to make sure there were no wild animals around, especially the one he heard and saw earlier.

Taking a careful look all around the mountain side, he still heard and saw nothing, taking another careful look, he took his time and tried to look into the forest, past the trees and bushes, he was looking for any kind of movement. Still, he didn't see any movement or hear any sound, just as he was about to enter the cave to put things away and get bear, he heard a growl, the sound was low and deep, not far away, standing there with the bowie in his hand he started to shake, looking all around again, he still didn't see anything, then he heard the growl, this time the sound came from behind him. Jimmy turned quickly and saw a brown bear. The bear had been lying behind a huge bush among a cluster of pine trees.

The bear was only a hundred and fifty feet away from Jimmy when he started running toward him, Jimmy knew he couldn't out run the bear, not on the side of this mountain, and from what he had seen on animal planet, he knew that bears could run faster than he, especially in their own domain, so he was going to have to fight.

Frank, Eileen and Jodie was just finishing breakfast when the doorbell rang, it was Detective Sgt. Collinsworth and his partner Detective Sgt. Joan Mathews, Frank bayed them to enter, sitting in the front room, Sgt. Collinsworth asked, "Has your son Jimmy returned home?" "No," Frank responded, "He hasn't, we formed a search party yesterday and looked all over town, in all directions with no results. We haven't started searching the country side yet, we plan to do that today." "Yes, I know, I have officer Suddeth's report." Frank, Eileen and Jodie listened while Sgt. Collinsworth and Sgt. Mathews went through the report Frank filled out at the police station, when they finished Sgt. Collinsworth asked if the report was correct, Frank said it was.

Frank and Eileen explained Jimmy's habits when he was upset, about leaving going around back then coming back in a few hours later. They always checked to see if he was there, he always was, except this time. They explained about the gold medallion and the argument they had with Jimmy, about his packing then leaving. How they waited for thirty minutes then checked on him, but this time he wasn't on the back patio. "Do you have a recent picture of Jimmy, you can have posters made up place them all over town, but before you start tacking them to telephone poles and putting them in store windows, you'll have to get a permit." "A permit," Eileen asked "Is that a new law just so the town can make more money, our son is missing, for all we know he could be dead. Is the city trying to make money from the death of a ten year old boy?"

"Mrs. Shannon, we don't know your boy is dead," said Sgt. Mathews, "We are here to help, to get all the information you can provide so we can inform not only our department, but the sheriff's office and the state troopers. We will form a search party and look for your son." "I'm sorry Sgt. It's just that I'm worried about him!" Eileen said as she started crying. "I know you are, it's only natural when something like this happens, parents are the most upset and worried, I promise we'll do everything we can to find Jimmy." "There is something else I need to tell you detective," Frank said, "A Mr. Boyle, from the newspaper called, he said the paper wanted to help, they're going to publish a story about Jimmy, and ask for their readers to help in the search. He is also going to call a team of men who search for missing and stranded people. He said they have a helicopter, he is going to ask them to help."

"I know the rescue team Mr. Boyle is talking about, there in Butte, and they are very good. I'm glad he's calling them they and a helicopter will be needed if we have to search these mountains. Thank you for telling us." said Sgt. Collinsworth. It was agreed a full scale search was called for. Sgt. Mathews was on the phone talking to the sheriff's department asking for their help, she then called the highway patrol office and asked them to inform their patrol units to keep an eye open for a ten year old boy by himself.

The bear that was charging toward Jimmy was a little more than a cub, maybe five or six months old, Jimmy didn't know what to do, facing the bear, he tried to scare the bear by yelling, waving his arms up and down, when that didn't work, Jimmy took hold of the bowie by the blade and thru it as hard as he could. When he threw the knife, he was holding it with the cutting edge toward his palm and sliced it open, he knew he was in a fight to the death, he knew it was that way with any wild animal, and paid no attention to the cut.

The knife spinning thru the air looked like a miss, before reaching Jimmy the bear stopped and started to rise up on his hind legs, the knife went thru the bears left eye. Growling, snorting in pain the bear raised up and faced Jimmy all the while losing blood, shaking his head vigorously trying to remove the knife from his eye. Jimmy couldn't wait any longer, with blood dripping from his hand he charged the bear, he was hoping he could get on the bears back, reach the knife, if he can, pull the knife out and stab the bear till he was dead.

Running toward the bear, Jimmy was also climbing up the hill so he would be above the bear, watching Jimmy closely the bear came down on all four, there was now only six or seven feet between them. The bear stood up on his hind legs, at the same time shaking his head, still trying to free the knife from his eye. Losing a lot of blood from shaking his head the bear was wearing down, Jimmy picked up a large rock, raising the rock over his head he heaved it as hard as he could, even though Jimmy was big for his age the rock was still heavy, being on higher ground he had the advantage, the rock hit the bear in his stomach knocking him off balance, falling backward the bear swung his arms franticly trying to remain up right, with nothing to grab hold of he fell backward tumbling and sliding down the hill.

The bear was on his right side, he stopped sliding and rolling down the steep mountain side when he hit a tree with his stomach, Jimmy was hurrying after him, he slipped on the wet pine needles and slid part way down, this was his chance, if he could get to the bear and pull the knife out, before he gets up he could stab him. When the bear slid into a tree he was sliding rather fast, it knocked the wind out of him, lying there on his right side breathing short breaths, gave Jimmy his opportunity.

Reaching the bear he jumped on it with his knees, putting one knee on the bears neck with all his weight, he pulled but the knife had cut into the skull bone, franticly, he see-sawed the knife back and forth, when it finally came free he placed the knife just behind the bears front leg, he pushed with all his might, the blade entered the bear up to the hilt. Penetrating his heart, Jimmy took a few steps back and waited. He watched the bear for a long time, trying to calm down, he told himself 'it's over, the bear is dead,' after a short while he made his way up the hill to the small cave to get his things, he kept looking over his shoulder to make sure the bear was not coming after him, inside the cave, he cut a strip of the blanket and wrapped it around his hand, he gathered up his things. The knife sheath was the kind that strapped around the leg and held on by velcro, picking up bear and the basket he left the cave making his way back down to where the bear laid dead.

Eileen took Jodie over to Kathleen, told her she would see her later that evening, they were going to look for Jimmy, "I hope you find him!" Jodie said, "I miss him." "Your dad and I miss him too sweetie, we'll do our best." Sgt. Collinsworth was put in charge of the search party, since word was out that Jimmy was missing, there were over three hundred people in the middle of town waiting for instructions.

The search and rescue team from Butte was there, the helicopter was on the ground at the west edge of town. Sgt. Collinsworth counted heads, then decided to have ten groups fan out in four different directions, the same as Mr. Shannon did the day before with four. The sky was clear and the breeze was warm, "We'll search until dark, each group go to your designated area and fan out, let's try to cover a large area today!" said Sgt. Collinsworth. The pilot of the helicopter was asked to search the mountains, as many as they could. To check all valleys and clearings, and the mountain sides.

At day's end all ten groups came up empty handed, two of the groups, the ones searching east and south had searched to the foot of the mountains, the north and west groups were still on the plains, they were told not to head toward the mountain. All ten groups had searched ten miles or more, when a few members of the south group got to the foot of the mountain they found no indication that he had been that way, no foot prints, or broken branches on bushes. They headed east skirting the mountain on the flats. Sgt. Collinsworth told them they would start the search again tomorrow morning at eight o'clock.

Jimmy approached the dead bear very slowly, when he was close enough he kick the bear, it didn't move, Jimmy kicked it again harder, still the bear didn't move, he put bear down out of the way, then he reached down and pulled the knife out, not knowing what to do next, he tried to pick the bear up but it was too heavy, then he remembered how the butchers at the super market cut up the beef. The beeves were just the body of the cows, no head and no inards or hide, Jimmy wanted the bear hide, it would help keep him and bear warm this winter. Getting hold of both hind legs he pulled the bear away from the tree, never having done this before he started cutting open the bear's stomach, he pulled out all the insides then cut them free, then he cut off the head. He tried picking it up again, it was still too heavy, he decided to drag it, after tying the twine thru the bears hind legs, he picked up bear and put him in the basket then he headed down the mountain.

Down on the lower side of the mountain Jimmy stopped to rest, he put the basket down and got bear out, he started playing with him, like all pups, bear was full of energy running around yipping, he would run up to Jimmy, then turn and run away, Jimmy laid down and bear ran to him, climb up on his stomach and licked his face, Jimmy started laughing, he petted bear, looking at him Jimmy saw blood on bear, he sat up then realized the blood on bear was coming from his hands. Putting bear back in the basket he started across the meadow, on the far side he came to a small spring with just a trickle of water.

He washed his hands and the knife, holding bear he rinsed the blood off him. Bear felt refreshed and started running around, rolling in the grass and yipping. Meanwhile Jimmy started skinning the bear, when he was done, he cut off a small piece to give to bear, smelling the meat first he took it and started eating. With no way to cook the meat, Jimmy tried a very small piece, he didn't like it but he was hungry so he ate it. With the taste of blood in his mouth he wanted to rinse it with water, but he was still hungry so he ate some more raw meat, when he was done he rinsed his mouth. That afternoon he found a place to spend the night, what he found was a place where five trees had fallen into a cluster like a lean-to, what caused them to fall he didn't know.

Jimmy started cutting big branches from bushes and placing them around the trees, he then cut branches off pine trees, the ones he could reach, he made sure they had a lot of pine needles on them, he placed his rain coat on top of the trees, then the branches, he placed them in different directions so if it rained he and bear could try to stay dry. The lean-to was just inside the tree line where the ground started slopping up. When he was done, he went back to the carcus bear was already chewing on it. Jimmy cut off another small piece and ate it. Sitting there looking around, he thought of the fight he had with the bear, 'I need to make some weapons, something I can use besides this knife' then he thought of his bow and arrows at home. "That's it," he said out loud, "I'll make a bow and some arrows." Looking around, he saw nothing he could use.

He spent the rest of the afternoon scraping the remnants of meat off the hide, placing the hide inside the lean-to where his bed was going to be, he then put the blanket on top of the hide. With his bed made, he went to hang up the meat. He cut the meat into four sections, carrying each section away from the lean-to he then tied one end of the twine to the meat, with the other end he climbed a tree and pulled the meat up and tied it to a higher branch.

After he tied the last section, he climbed down, he wanted to check the cut on his hand, his right hand was hurting, he didn't know if it was bleeding or not, he didn't see any blood. At the small creek he unwrapped his hand, looking at it he saw it was swollen, and was red all around the cut, but it wasn't bleeding. He carefully washed his hands. He then held his right hand in the icy water. While he was soaking his hand, he took the soiled bandage and rinsed it best he could. When his hand was cold, he removed it from the water, he rubbed it gently to warm it, putting it back into the water, he repeated this several times.

Finally he stood up, taking the other strip of blanket he used as a bandage from his left rear pocket, he wrapped his hand. Back at the lean-to, he put the rinsed blanket bandage over a branch to dry. It was twilight now the sun had gone down behind the mountain. Looking around for bear he didn't see him. 'BEAR' he called out, standing in front of the lean-to, he heard a whimper, it was coming from inside, turning he saw bear lying on the blanket looking at him.

He chuckled as he entered the lean-to, "Ready for bed bear?" he said, "I don't blame you, it has been a long day!" Jimmy sat on the blanket holding and petting bear, his thoughts wondered back home, thinking about Jodie, he hoped she was okay. He wanted to see her and talk to her, to let her know he too was okay. Then his thoughts turned to his parents.

'If I ever see them again, I won't know what to say maybe it would be best not to say anything, let them talk first, or do I even want to see them. I do want to see Jodie and if the only way I can see and talk to her is to talk to them, I will.' By now it was dark, Jimmy wasn't sleepy, he was just tired, still holding and petting bear, he noticed bear was asleep. He sat quiet in the lean-to listening to all the night sounds, he heard crickets chirping by the little creek, he heard other sounds he couldn't identify, then off in the distance he heard a wolf howling, it sounded far away.

He knew the night creatures were out looking for food. The front of the lean-to was wide open, and being pitch black he knew he couldn't find any branches to cover it, he was starting to get scared, there was a slight breeze, it could send his and bears scent a long ways. 'Should I stay awake all night, will it be safe if I go to sleep' he was thinking. He decided to stay awake. A few hours later he could hardly keep his eyes open, the next thing he knew it was morning, he don't remember falling asleep, he looked for bear, hoping he didn't wonder off and wasn't taken during the night. Bear was growing, he wasn't a little pup anymore, Jimmy saw a small bulge in the blanket at the foot of his bed, he poked it and it moved.

Removing the blanket, he saw bear all curled up, Jimmy was happy now, his friend didn't wonder off and he wasn't taken. I'm not alone. "Well bear," he said, "Are you hungry?" Jimmy sat there looking out over the clearing, what he could of it, from that angle he didn't see any other animals, then he turned to his left, looking through the cracks, over and under the fallen trees, keeping a close watch for anything that moved, nothing, he then turned to his right and repeated the process, looking through the trees and into the rest of the clearing. He still didn't see anything, that didn't mean there wasn't some animal out there that he couldn't see.

Not seeing anything or any animal that could be a danger to him or bear, Jimmy left the lean-to, he went to where the meat was hanging and looked up, there were only three sections there, only the twine was left of the forth, tied to the branch, he checked all around, he didn't find any tracks, or where the meat hit the ground, what he did find was claw marks on the tree. A mountain lion he guessed, he wanted to gather up his things and head south, but he had to be sure which way the cat went, he didn't want to run into it later.

Checking the area, he walked all around, back and forth he went searching the ground, half way across the clearing to the north he saw a bear spot with very few weeds or grass, approaching the spot he saw tracks, looking at them, he guessed they were made by the mountain lion, they were big and heading north. 'Good,' he thought. 'Now we can eat, and be on our way.' An hour later Jimmy and bear had eaten, he filled all four bottles with water, everything was packed, tied up or hung on his back and they were on their way.

Chapter Eight

For the next two weeks, the search party came up empty, they didn't find any trace of Jimmy, no footprints, no broken branches, no pieces of clothing, nothing, and no one they had talked to had seen him, they had even walked the fence on both sides of every highway leading out of town from the edge of town for ten miles looking for anything that might be his or where he crossed thru, still nothing. The helicopter that was searching the mountains all around Billings also came up empty.

As a last resort, the sheriff went to the local Indian tribe and talked to the tribal council. He told them the story about Jimmy being missing, and the result of their search. Sherriff John Macklin asked the tribal council for help, asking if some of their men could take a few days to look for Jimmy, that maybe they could find something that the others could not.

The tribal council told sheriff Macklin that it would be impossible because the heavy rain these past few weeks would have erased most if not all signs that Jimmy might have left. "Yes, I understand," said Macklin, "I am asking you to please try, the boy's parents are really upset and worried they fear the boy is dead." "That is a good possibility, if he has disappeared without a trace, anything could have happened!" said chief Running Bull (His Christian name is Joseph Blackstone) "This is true, that's why I am asking for your help," Macklin replied. Falling White star (Christian name, Jack Spencer) one of the tribal elders asked "What was the boy wearing when he disappeared?

Sheriff Macklin replied "His parents told me Jimmy was wearing jeans, shirt, work boots and a clear rain coat, in his backpack he had two pair of jeans, two shirts, two pair of sox and a winter coat along with a few other things." "What other things?" Joseph asked. "Some twine, a ball of string, and a pocket knife," said the Sheriff. The tribal council decided to help. "We will try, but we make no promises, I will assign four men to look in all directions, they will trace your steps outside of town. Tell the boy's parents we will look for one week, if nothing is found, the boy is gone!"

During the two weeks the others were looking for him, Jimmy had made his way south, at the end of the second week working his way up and down mountains, across valleys and clearings Jimmy had traveled a long way. One day, he had just crossed a clearing and was among the trees when he heard a motor. It didn't sound like a vehicle so he watched the sky, when he saw the helicopter it was flying low, just above the tree tops and it was moving slow. 'They are looking for me' he was thinking, 'I can't let them find me.' He hid behind a huge bush near a cluster of pine tree's he stayed there till the helicopter left.

When it was gone he made his way south along the bottom, staying in among the trees, just in case the helicopter came back. While he was walking he kept trying to remember what he saw on one of those programs on TV that showed how to make a bow and arrows. It also showed how to shoot a bow and arrow accurately, the second segment was how to rig a snare to catch a rabbits or any kind of small game and so on. Then he remembered it was a program on survival.

During those same two weeks, he and bear had eaten the bear he killed, now they had no food, sometimes he had been lucky, he was able to snare a few rabbits. There also were days he and bear had to go hungry, sometimes two or three days at a time. When he was able to snare a rabbit he saved the skins, but he still didn't like the taste of raw meat but with no way to cook it he made himself eat it. The milk, the cup cakes and fruit were gone long ago, the four water bottles he kept. He could refill them when he came to a creek, if the water was clear.

By midafternoon one day he and bear topped a ridge, looking around in all directions, he wondered what day it was, he didn't know, he didn't even know, what month it was. Was it still July, maybe it was August? All he could see was more mountains, each one was a different shade of green, from the green of the pine trees to the other shades of the oak, aspen, and maple, the closest mountain was the brightest, the farther away they were the darker, the farther ones looked almost black. Since it was mid-afternoon, he knew it would be dark soon so he had to find a place to stay the night, he also knew it would be warmer at the bottom of a mountain.

The afternoon chill made him hurry, carrying the basket in his left hand and bear under his coat on the right side he partly ran, and slid down the hill, the downhill side was steeper, sliding downhill on his butt he looked ahead, he saw that the pine trees ended and there was clear sky. Not realizing it was a drop off, he wasn't taking any chances, he let go of the basket and grabbed for some bush branches, not being able to hold on and the edge getting closer, he rolled to his right, that put him in the path of a big pine tree, he hit the tree with the bottom of his feet to stop, he put his left arm around the tree to hold on.

Breathing hard and scared of what could have happened, he checked to see if bear was alright, opening his coat a little he looked down at bear, "You okay bear," he asked, bear whimpered, "I know bear, I'm hungry to. I have to find a place to stay!" Getting to his feet, he carefully made his way and retrieved the basket. Jimmy inched his way toward the edge of the cliff, peeking over the edge, he could see the bottom, it was at least three hundred feet straight down, looking right and left he saw a long wide valley, off to his right on the valley floor he saw a creek.

The creek angled its way southeast from the cliff. He wondered where the water was coming from. He hadn't seen a creek or even heard running water. Turning right he worked his way among the trees and brush till he heard running water. Carefully and slowly, he moved till he came to the creek. First his eyes followed the creek up the mountain till it disappeared, "No wonder I didn't hear running water," he said out loud, "I came from the other way." Then he turned his attention to the cliff, easing his way to where the water went over the edge, he looked down and saw the water fall, he also saw the pond the water splashed into and from there made its way southeast.

The water fall created a mist, when the sun peeked out from behind a cloud and shined down on the valley, along with a slight breeze, Jimmy could see the red, green, and yellow colors of a rainbow. The light breeze had also made the cliff wall wet, now he has to look for a way down, not seeing one. "Well bear, which way shall we go?" he asked.

Jimmy decided to go left, he had gone maybe a quarter of a mile, working his way up the hill away from the edge, trying to hold onto bear and keep clear of the edge on this steep mountain side, he could only use one hand, at times he would need both. Standing on the up side of a tree, using it for support, he thought if he tied the twine around his waist tight enough where he was holding onto bear, then bear wouldn't fall out the bottom and he could use both hands. He sat down took off the backpack and looked thru it till he found the twine, placing the basket on his right side he put the twine thru the handle, tying it tightly around his waist on the outside of his coat, he used the bowie to cut the excess.

Ready to go again, he stood up, holding on to the tree he jumped up several times to make sure bear wouldn't fall out the bottom of his coat, "Ready to go bear?" he asked. As he was making his way up and down the hill, around trees and bushes and sometimes thru them he was hoping he could make it to the valley floor before dark. An hour later, with the sun low in the western sky, it had disappeared behind the mountain he was on. Jimmy knew it would be dark soon and he still hasn't found a way down. "Well bear," he said, "We'll have to find a place up here where it's cold and fined a way down to the valley floor in the morning."

He climbed up and down along the mountain side for another hour when he saw two thin pine trees that had fallen parallel to each other, the two trees, when they fell got lodged in some thicker branches of other trees and were on a steep angle, checking them out he noticed a few foot prints on the up side of where the trees had once stood, looking at the prints, he saw they were huge, flat with five toes, animal planet came to his mind again and on one program he saw, it showed the different shapes of wild animals hooves and paw prints, from that, he knew these prints were of a large bear and that he, she or they pushed these trees over. He didn't know how old the prints were or even if the bear or bears were still in the area, but he had no choice, it was getting darker, and the sun no longer shone. Untying the twine, he let the basket fall as he held onto bear. Putting bear in the basket he placed it on the upside of a nearby tree out of the way.

"Well bear, I guess we'll have to stay here tonight, I'll try to fix this up for us, you, stay in the basket!" Jimmy searched the area for other smaller logs he could carry or drag, also some thick branches that are lying on the ground, he had to make another lean-to and he knew he didn't have much time before it would be too dark to see. By the time it was too dark to see he was just finishing, he would have been done a little sooner except bear playing in the basket tipped it over and wondered off, when Jimmy saw he was gone, he went looking for him. "BEAR, WHERE ARE YOU, BEAR, C'MERE BOY," he heard bear make a small high pitch sound about thirty yards up the mountain side, climbing up to him, he picked bear up, petted him, tickled him under his chin, "You know you shouldn't wonder off like that!"

Joseph Blackstone (Chief Running Bull) asked to have all the men gather on the ground in front of the council lodge, within the hour all the men were present, he told them that a ten year old boy was missing, and that the sheriff was asking for their help, he wanted four volunteers to look for him. He picked the first four men who raised their hands. Asking them to step forward, he handed one of them a picture the sheriff had of Jimmy, he told them to look for one week, one man will look north and east, one man will look east and south, one man will look south and west, the fourth man will look west and north, that way there will be two men searching the same quarter of the compass. Each man will take his pick-up, horse trailer, and two horses, with enough food and water supply to last the week, they are to search as if they were tracking a wild animal, to check every print, every broken blade of grass or stick and twig.

Sheriff Macklin went to the Shannon resident to inform Mr. and Mrs. Shannon that four men of the tribe was going to look for Jimmy on horseback, he explained the instructions of Mr. Blackstone, and told them that they would search continually for one week, if they came up empty that means Jimmy is gone, and the only thing left is to search as much as possible to try to find his body. When sheriff Macklin said 'find his body' Eileen broke down, she couldn't help it, she cried out loud, shaking in fear.

When the sheriff left, Eileen started yelling, "WHAT IN THE HELL DID WE DO, WE ACCUSED JIMMY OF BEING A THIEF AND A LIAR AND WE JUST LET HIM WALK OUT OF HERE." Frank tried to stay calm so he could calm Eileen down, he talked to her in a quiet tone, "Eileen, you have to calm down, we don't know that Jimmy is gone, never give up hope, we'll keep looking, he has to be around here somewhere. "DAMMIT FRANK, WE LOOKED EVERYWHERE AROUND HERE, SEVERAL TIMES, OVER TWO HUNDRED PEOPLE LOOKED FOR HIM FOR TWO WEEKS, IF HE WAS AROUND HERE DON'T YOU THINK WE WOULD HAVE FOUND HIM?" Jodie was sitting at the kitchen table when her mother started yelling, the second time her mother started yelling she didn't want to hear it, getting up from the table Jodie ran upstairs to her room, she slammed the door and locked it. She got in bed, pulled the blankets over her head and she to, started crying, "Oh Jimmy where are you, you can't be dead, I love you"

One week later, the four men returned from their search and reported to Mr. Blackstone, they told him about the search, Mr. Blackstone then called sheriff Macklin and asked him to meet them at the Shannon home in one hour, he then called Mr. and Mrs. Shannon and informed them that his men were back from the search and asked if they could come over to explain in one hour. The Shannon's were very nervous. Mr. Blackstone and Mr. Haley arrived first, the sheriff arrived five minutes later. Frank heard the car doors shut so he met them at the front door, when they were all seated at the kitchen table, Jodie was sitting on her mother's lap, they were both jittery not knowing the news. Eileen got up to make coffee, Jodie sat in the chair. Frank, the sheriff and the two tribesmen sat around the table waiting for Eileen, when she was seated.

Mr. Dale Haley (Black Wolf) started talking, since he was one of the men on the search, sheriff and Mr. Blackstone agreed he should be the one to tell the Shannon's. "Mr. Mrs. Shannon, my name is Dale Haley, I am also called Black Wolf, I was one of four looking for your son, the other three found no sign of your son, but I did." "You found him?" Eileen asked excitedly, "No ma-am, I said, I found sign of him, what I found was two foot prints, when I saw them I got off my horse to make sure, they were the prints of work shoes of young boy, the prints showed he was headed up into the mountains. There is a dirt road west of town that only goes up to the mountains that is the trail he took, I followed his trail from the road to the mountain. Even with all the rain, he left a trail he did not try to hide himself. It now has been three weeks, if he is up in those mountains, it will be hard to find him. Once in the mountains he may try to hide his tracks, if he does, we will never find him." "Mr. Haley, you believe Jimmy went up into those mountains, if he did, do you think you could find him?" asked Eileen.

"I don't know Mrs. Shannon," Mr. Haley said, "Those mountains are very dangerous, they are very steep, they also have drop offs or cliffs, the forest is also very thick, pine needles and leaves on the ground don't tell much, a person can walk thru the forest and not leave a trail." "But will you try?" She asked, "I will pay you whatever you want, I just want my son back." "I truly understand how you feel, I would feel the same way if one of my sons was missing, but Mrs. Shannon, I would have to go up there on foot as your son did, it would take me a long time to cover any ground, I have to look for sign he may have left." "I'm begging you to try. I will pay all your expense, and pay you to, PLEASE Mr. Haley, I beg you."

"Alright, Mrs. Shannon, I will try, it might help to go faster if I took another tracker with me, four eyes are better than two!" "Oh yes," she said, "I leave it up to you, let your partner know I will pay him to." "Mrs. Shannon, I don't want your money, I do this for your son, I can only guess how scared he is, up there all alone, not to mention the wild animals. You pay for supplies that will be enough." "Yes of course I will, when can you get started?" "We can start in two day's it will take that long to get things together."

Thank you Mr. Haley, I wish you and your partner the best of luck." "Thank you, I will let you know what we find, if anything." "How much will your supplies cost?" she asked. "For the two of us . . . , for one week . . . , about a hundred dollars each will do it. We can also take some supplies from home." "Frank," she said, "Write Mr. Haley a check for one thousand dollars, I insist on paying him and his partner for helping to find Jimmy!"

"Mrs. Shannon, I told you I don't want your money, I'm . . . ." "Mr. Haley, please except it, I can't imagine what you will be going through looking for Jimmy, but I must compensate you for what you are doing for us. Will that be enough?" "Yes ma'am! That will be enough." After the three men left, Eileen was more joyful, more hopeful, she was even smiling. "You seem to be in a good mood!" Frank said. "Yes I am," she replied, "You heard what Mr. Haley said, he found Jimmy's foot prints that means we know which way he went. He's up in those mountains."

"Yes, but we still haven't found him, anything can happen up there." Eileen turned on him, she had an evil look on her face, raising her voice again she said, "DAMMIT FRANK, CAN'T YOU EVER THINK POSITIVE? YOUR NOT GOING TO RUIN IT FOR ME THIS TIME. I BELIEVE JIMMY IS STILL ALIVE, IF HE IS, MR. HALEY WILL FIND, HIM." "I only ment . . . ." Frank tried to reply. "I KNOW WHAT YOU MEANT, FOR THREE WEEKS NOW WE HAVE SEARCHED EVERYWHERE EXCEPT, THOSE MOUNTAINS, THAT'S WHERE HE WENT, AND THAT'S WHERE WE'LL FIND HIM!" "Eileen, you don't have to shout, and for your information, I do believe Jimmy is still alive and I won't believe differently until it is proven otherwise."

Chapter Nine

Having a restless night, Jimmy could only doze, he tried to sleep but the foot prints he saw of a huge bear and the fight he had with a midsize brown bear some days ago worried him, the cold night didn't help much, each time he woke up he would check on bear (The wolf Pup), bear didn't seem to have a worry in the world, he was sound asleep. The make-shift lean-to Jimmy constructed didn't help to keep out the cold or the wind he also thought sleeping uphill didn't help either. The night was cold and quiet, the light wind blowing through the pines made a whispering sound, in a way it was soothing and in another it worried him, he couldn't hear if a wild animal were around until it was close, then it might be too late.

Jimmy was glad when it was finally daylight, when dawn came he stayed in the lean-to looking through the cracks all around, he didn't see or hear any animals, he decided to go out and look around, he was satisfied all was clear. Putting the blanket in the basket and then bear, he rolled the bear skin, using the twine he tied the hide to one side of the handle. When he picked up the basket bear was looking at him, "Well bear," he said, "Let's see if we can get down to the valley floor today, maybe we can find something to eat."

Heading east along the edge which curved around toward the southeast, he still stayed away from it, trying to find a way down, making his way through the thickness of trees and bushes, by midmorning he stopped, "Look there bear," he laughed, "the drop off ends, it goes into the mountain, that's where we can go down." Wanting to hurry, he knew he had to be careful not to slip. It took a little more than an hour but finally reaching the bottom, he walked south again toward the water fall, there he took bear out of the basket and let it drop, looking up he said, "Wow, that's a long drop!" He put bear down so he could run and play while he attended to the cut on his palm, cutting another strip from the blanket, he went to the creek, unwrapping his hand slowly it started hurting, looking at it, the cut went all the way across his palm.

He soaked his hand in the cold running water, it felt good, washing the dry blood off he rewrapped his hand then rinsed the other strip of blanket to use again, now to look for something to eat he found more of those wild onions and turnips around the pond and along the creek banks on both sides. The grass was a dark green with some wild flowers and a few willow trees, Bear ran toward the grass, his little legs moving forty miles an hour, he let out a little growl, jumping, running, and rolling. Jimmy watched and laughed at bears antics.

He washed the off the wild vegetables then decided to make a bow and some arrows, eating while he worked he first got the string out of his backpack to measure it's length holding one end in his left hand, he stretched the sting out tight with his right, with a lot of slack left, he doubled it then stretched it out again, his arms weren't straight out when he held both ends tight, "That's long enough," he said to himself, "Now to find a good branch of willow for the bow, and some straight branches for arrows."

Being on the north side of the creek, he went to those willows first, he found what he was looking for using the string he measured the branch plus three inches on each end. With the bowie knife he cut branch off at the bottom, dragged it to where he could work on it, cutting off all the smaller branches flush he then measured the length using the string, then he peeled the bark off. When he was done, he stood there holding it in his right hand, "Wow," he thought, "This will make a good staff!" While he was working he was also thinking that the only one he had to talk to was bear and since bear couldn't talk there was no need for him to talk either. He could train bear by using hand signals. From then on he never spoke another word. When he thought that he caught movement off to his right. Turning he saw a rabbit.

Once again animal planet popped into Jimmy's mind, (Survival, How to catch small wild game), Jimmy wondered what to do, he searched the creek bank, looking for anything a rabbit might eat, what he found was something that looked like a baby carrot, he rinsed it in the creek, took a small bite, immediately spitting it out, it was sour and didn't taste good, using his knife he cut off a piece of turnip. Using some string and twine tied together, he tied one end to a stick, the other end he made a loop with a slip knot, going to where he saw the rabbit, using a rock he pounded the stick in the ground, laid out the string and placed the piece of turnip in the middle. Back at the creek with bear, he played with the wolf pup for a while, tickling, petting and rolling with him, they both seemed to be happy, Jimmy laughing, bear whining and growling having a good time. He also tried to teach him some hand signals, his right hand out with palm down, he did this several times. He decided to train bear using one signal at a time.

After a while, Jimmy got back to business, searching the willow trees for straight branches, he didn't see any on these trees, but the two trees on the other side of the creek he saw a few that looked straight, at the creeks bank he stopped, taking off his boots and sox, he thought, 'I haven't had a bath since I left home." He decided to wash not only himself, but his clothes to. Picking up his sox he waded into the water, it was ice cold, then he sat down, the water was knee deep, he rubbed his sox together, rung them out, did it again, then he threw them on the bank, removing his shirt he did the same, then off came his pants, rubbing them together up and down using the legs, he threw them on the bank, he then washed his under ware.

Now that he was naked he washed himself, first his arms then his legs, he washed his stomach, chest, shoulders and as much of his back as he could reach, then his face, with his hands cupped with water he wet his hair, must it up, then repeated it several times, done bathing he left the creek, he picked up his close placing them on a nearby bush. The temperature in the valley was a lot warmer than on the mountain, the sun was also warmer, with little breeze up close to the cliff he hoped his close would be dry before dark.

Standing there naked he thought 'If I stay in the mountains for a long time, I will outgrow my clothes then what will I do? Maybe I can make something.' glancing at the snare nothing, he had to find a place to stay the night, he liked it here in this valley, he and bear might stay a few days if he can find something to eat. He crossed the creek and went toward the trees with knife in hand, finding five straight branches he started cutting, he had cut three when he suddenly stopped, he couldn't believe it, 'Is that a hole in the wall?' he wondered. Before going to check it out, he thought of all kinds possibilities of what it might be or what could be in there, is it a cave or just a hole in the wall, if it's a cave what lives in it, a bear or a mountain lion or some other kind of wild animal, a pack of wolves maybe.

In order to get near the falls, Jimmy had to enter the pond. The pond itself was a thirty foot circle of sort. It was also almost waist deep on Jimmy from the years the water had poured over the cliff. Carefully Jimmy entered the pond, trying not to make too much noise, 'this is stupid' he thought, 'if there is any wild animal in there, it would have heard us by now, as much noise as bear and I made playing and me chopping wood,' still he wanted to be careful just in case. Wading across the pond with bowie in hand, he saw that it was a cave, the opening was behind the falls, that's why he didn't see till now, on the south side of the pond, the cave opening was receded more than the north side, but still it can't be seen unless a person is next to the willow trees which is next to the wall, and the water blocked the opening.

Back on the reservation, Mr. Haley asked his friend Mr. Fred Hanney (Tatopa) if he would help track the boy, explaining everything up to date his friend agreed. Mr. Blackstone approved, they made all arrangements for the week then gathered all their gear and packed winter clothing for the trip. They each were going to take hand guns and 30-30 rifles, just in case, on the second day they were ready to go. Mr. Haley called Mrs. Shannon he told her they were ready except for a few groceries and ammunition for their rifles, she told Mr. Haley she would meet them at the store. After paying for their supplies, she wished them both, good luck. On her way home she knew this was going to be a long week of waiting. Mrs. Haley went with them to drive the truck back home, at the foot of the mountain, Dale and Fred strapped on their side arm, put their packs on their backs and pick up their rifles, Mr. Haley kissed his wife bye.

It was ten thirty am on the second day when Dale and Fred started up the mountain, while they climbed, they look for foot prints, slide marks, broken branches or any other kind of sign Jimmy might have left. Half way up the mountain they found where Jimmy had slipped twice. One piece of equipment Fred brought with him was a camera he took two pictures of the marks Jimmy had left. At the top of the mountain among the rocks and boulders, they found where Jimmy had spent the night by the muddy foot prints entering the cave. Taking out a pad and pencil,

Dale wrote what they had found up to this point. Fred took pictures of where Jimmy had spent the night. "Jimmy didn't leave much of a trail, did he?" Dale asked. "No, he hides his trail well. If he keeps hiding his trail, we may not find him." Fred said. "Maybe not, we will do our best!" Dale and Fred followed Jimmy's trail for three days, they found where he slept each night, Dale noted every detail of their search, he also noted how Jimmy secured the place he spent each night. Fred took pictures of everything they found.

When they found the hole in the ground, they both looked inside, saw where Jimmy had slept, saw the cut branches, they also saw the foot prints of a small dog or a wolf pup. Dale made a note of this while Fred took some pictures. Then they saw the blood, and how the blood had a spray pattern, they figured Jimmy had gotten into a fight with a wild animal. Dale picked up the blood from several different places and placed them in a plastic bag. Looking around they finally saw where the wild animal had tumbled and slid down the hill, and the skid mark Jimmy made going it. They also found a big rock with a bloody hand print on it. They knew it had to be Jimmies blood so they decided to take the rock back with them. Since they were documenting what they find for Mrs. Shannon, Fred took pictures of everything on the side of the mountain, from foot prints to where he slept in the hole and the skid marks.

It was after he sealed the plastic bag, that Dale looked down the hill and saw a huge black area by a tree, "Fred," Dale said, "Look down there." pointing to the black area, Fred looked, "MY GOD! Do you think . . ." "I don't know, we better check it out." "Yeah," sliding down the mountain side they stopped before they reached the area, they didn't want to disturb anything before taking pictures. They repeated the same procedure Fred took pictures and Dale bagged some of the blood, since there was more of it, he bagged more. When they were done they looked around for any remains, there was none. No bones, no guts and no head. No nothing.

What they did find was a lot of paw prints of all kinds of animals, bear, wolves, mountain lions, and other scavengers, as well as bird foot prints, and a lot of scuff marks. "Do you think . . . this was Jimmy?" Fred asked, as he took pictures of the paw and scrapping marks. "I don't know . . . there's enough blood to be him." Dale commented. "If it was him, he had one hell of a fight with whatever animal attacked him." Fred said. "He sure did," Dale answered, "But we don't know if it's him, let's look around, maybe we'll find something."

Dale and Fred searched the surrounding area for a hundred yards in every direction, they couldn't find any more foot prints or skid marks. It seemed the trail ended there. Any marks Jimmy made during the fight were near the hole and at the tree, during the two weeks from the time of the incident to now other animals had covered them over. There were no prints or skid marks of any kind going farther down the mountain side. "Well Dale, this is where his trail ends, what do you think?" "What do I think? I think Jimmy is dead." "Do you want to keep looking?" asked Fred. "We have been looking for three days his trail has brought us here. We have searched the area and found nothing, only the prints of animals and birds. This is a lot of blood, as much as a small person has, what else can we conclude, except he is dead." said Dale. "That is terrible news to take to his parents!" "Yes it is, we have no choice, his trail ends here and his trail is cold.

"Well, we have the blood samples from here, and up there and we have this rock that has blood all over it and the hand print, the sheriff can send them to the lab to see who's blood it is!" "I guess that's all we can do since there is no more trail. If Jimmy is gone, I wonder what kind of animal he had to fight." Dale asked. "That is something we will never know, he was very brave for a ten year old boy, fighting a wild animal knowing it was kill or be killed." "Yes he was," said Dale, "Let's go home."

It took Dale and Fred two days to get back to Billings since they didn't have to look for signs. Standing on top of the mountain overlooking Billings Dale took out his cell phone, called his wife, he asked her to pick them up that they would be waiting for her by the road. It was ten forty five am on the third day that they walked into the sheriff's office. They had been gone five days. In the outer office, they told the deputy they would like to see Sheriff Macklin, "Tell him it's about Jimmy Shannon!" a few minutes later they were sitting in front the Sheriff's desk explaining what they found, "Sheriff, I took notes of everything we found, and Fred took pictures. We brought this rock, as you can see, it has blood on it, and we believe this hand print is Jimmy's. We have to get the film developed but here is what we found that I noted." said Dale.

Sheriff Macklin read the list of notes Dale had given him, "MY GOD, is Jimmy dead?" "We don't know that for sure Sheriff, said Dale," I only wrote down what we found, we didn't find any remains, no close, no shoes, no body parts, nothing, only a lot of blood, A LOT OF BLOOD, we searched the area very carefully for a hundred yards in all directions, there was no more signs, only animal tracks." "Dale is right," said Fred "I asked him if we should search some more, but neither of us knew which way to go. The mountain side was steep where we found the blood, If Jimmy was alive and won the fight, he would of left a trail, there was none." "FIGHT WHAT FIGHT?" asked Macklin.

Dale replied, "From the way it looked, where we found the blood, there had to be one hell of a fight, it started about thirty yards above where the largest amount of blood was, I guess it ended at the pool of blood. We have pictures of the whole area including foot prints of a boy and some animals. My guess is that Jimmy fought with a bear!" "HOLY SH . . . ." said Macklin, "What are we going to tell his parent's?" "We tell them the truth," replied Fred, "We don't know if Jimmy is dead or alive, we'll have to wait for the results of the blood test, and we have to get this film developed.

While Dale, Fred and the sheriff was still talking, Mr. Blackstone arrived, entering the sheriff's office he told the deputy who he was and was taken to the sheriff's office. Half hour later Sheriff Macklin and Mr. Blackstone knew the whole story, every detail, Jimmy's treck up and down the mountains, where he stayed each night, up to and including the fight. The only thing they didn't know for sure was bear (the wolf pup). All they knew was that they had pictures of a small animal they decided it had to be a wolf pup. "Well Sheriff, we have to explain this to Mr. and Mrs. Shannon. I think it would be best if we all went to tell them." Mr. Blackstone said. "I think so," Macklin said, "But I sure don't envy the job of being the bearer of bad news. Let me tell my deputies in charge of evidence to box up the rock and blood samples and send it to the lab, then we can go, we can stop on the way to the Shannon's to get the film developed, the camera shop now has a one hour developing machine!"

Chapter Ten

The falling water was cold, and Jimmy knew he was going to get wet, making not a sound he carefully went behind the falls to the opening, slowly he inched his way up a few steps till he could see into the cave, he looked for any kind of animal moving or lying down, he also looked for shining eyes and listened for any kind of sound, he saw or heard neither one, he moved in closer till he was standing in the mouth of the opening. The opening to the cave was twice as tall as Jimmy, stretching out his arms, he could not touch both walls, looking into the cave, he could only see about thirty or forty feet into it, the surface floor was relatively smooth with a few bumps, there were also some rocks and boulders scattered around, slowly he started walking deeper into the cave, ready to turn and run if he had to. After walking a few feet he would stop and listen again, he listened for any kind of sound, a growl, a hiss, a scratching sound, a whimper, a thud as if something was walking toward him, but he heard nothing.

'I wish I had a flashlight', he thought, 'Then, I wouldn't have to be so scared.' He was twenty feet into the cave, standing there he tried to see further back into the cave but it was too dark, he still didn't hear any noise, looking toward the falls, the light from outside and the sun shining on the water fall dimly illuminated the immediate area. The shadows on the cave walls and from the boulders were a little scary, then he thought of spiders, big spiders or maybe even snakes hiding in the shadows. He also noticed it was a lot warmer in the cave than outside, but the nights are still going to be cold, he had the bear skin to lie on, and the blanket to cover him and bear.

He decided to go back outside and work on making arrows, outside as he was wading across the pond to pick up the sticks he cut, he looked all over the valley making sure there were no animals near, looking to the north, he saw nothing, he didn't see bear either. Sticks in hand, he headed to the narrower part of the creek, crossing over he saw bear curled up near a willow tree sound asleep. It was noon, the sun high in the sky, on the north side of the creek he decided he was going to look for stone arrow heads and feathers, he saw a few feathers here and there on the ground but they were too small. Then he found a black and white Eagle feather, he picked it up, looking at it, he liked it, it was a long one, when he got back to the creek he would wash it and tie it to his hair.

The rocks he looked at he didn't like, they were too thick, not shaped right or had no way to tie them to the arrow, while he was walking around, eyes glued to the ground, he noticed some movement from the corner of his eye, something moved, turning his head, he saw a rabbit stuck in the snare. The rabbit was jumping, squirming and pulling, trying to get loose, Jimmy ran over, picking up the string he pulled it tight, the rabbit fighting trying to be free, but in the end he lost. The string was around the rabbit's neck, when Jimmy picked him up off the ground, he had no more leverage, the rabbit just hung there kicking.

Jimmy, with the bowie in his hand stabbed the rabbit in the stomach as hard as he could, the knife went all the way threw, freeing the rabbit from the string he carried it a long way from the pond before he cleaned and skinned it, back at the pond he washed it then cut the rabbit meat into thin strips, he and bear ate. Some of the thin strips he cut into smaller pieces for bear. Jimmy didn't like eating raw rabbit any more than he did raw bear, but he was hungry and he managed to eat enough to curb the hunger feeling.

After eating, he and bear both felt a lot better, bear started running around in circles yipping and growling, Jimmy on his hands and knees chased bear, catching each other, Jimmy rolled over on his back, bear at his side, Jimmy pulled him up onto his stomach, bear walked onto his chest and started licking his face, tail just a wagging, Jimmy was laughing as he petted him. After a short while playing with bear, he turned his attention to finding feathers and arrow heads. With bear following he walked slowly so bear could keep up. Going south across the valley, Jimmy continued to look till the sun was low, working his way back to the falls, he did find a few feathers big enough for his arrows. When they reached the pond bear was tired.

Jimmy decided to wait till tomorrow to work on his arrows, right now he had to get his close, shoes, backpack, blanket, basket and bear into the cave and make camp. Putting everything in the basket, he took it over to the cave then came back for bear. Putting the branches for the bow and arrows by the tree, he picked up bear, waded across the creek and pond again. Inside the cave, not too far from the entrance he spread his rain coat, the bear skin, then his blanket, the remaining parts of the rabbit, which were the two hind legs he put in the basket with his close. Bear came to his side, it would be dark before long, Jimmy covered them both with the blanket soon they were both sound asleep.

Sheriff Macklin and the other three men decided to have lunch after dropping off the film, they thought it best to have the pictures to show to Mr. and Mrs. Shannon when they explain what they found, along with the notes, they could explain the pictures better, they were to be satin finished pictures 8 x 10'S, Fred had taken the whole role, 36 exposures, when lunch was over and they had picked up the pictures, the four men looked at them, then Dale put them in order, starting from the first sign Jimmy left to where the huge pool of blood laying on the ground. The last four pictures were of the area of the side of the mountain where the fight had started, the trees, bushes, some rocks of all sizes scattered and the sprayed blood on the rocks and ground, Dale kneeling on one knee pointing to the blood. The last picture showed him pointing to the skid marks and the huge pool of blood.

At the Shannon home, Frank was outside watering the flowers and bushes along the front of the house, sheriff Macklin pulled into the driveway, Joseph Blackstone parked on the street, Frank turned off the water, the five men shook hands then went into the house, Eileen and Jodie was watching TV, when Eileen saw them she turned the TV off, stood up quickly, looking at Dale, her heart started pounding faster and she tried to read his expression, he had a sad look. "Do you have news, Mr. Haley?" she asked nervously, sheriff Macklin spoke up quickly, "Mr., Mrs. Shannon, I think it would be best if we talked privately!" "You have bad news?" asked frank.

"Please, Mr. Shannon, what we have to talk about would be best if your daughter wasn't here, you can explain to her later!" Dale told them. "Jodie please go to your room and close the door," "Mom, I want to hear about Jimmy!" "Jodie you heard your mother, go to your room and close the door, we will talk to you later about Jimmy." "You promise?" she asked. "Yes dear, we promise." Her mother answered. "Let's go in the kitchen," Eileen then said, "I'll put on some coffee." In the kitchen, all five men were seated at the table, no one spoke till Eileen had made coffee and was seated. In front of Dale was a manila envelope and a note pad, Mr. and Mrs. Shannon knew they had news, they didn't know if the news was good or bad.

"Mr. Haley," Frank asked, opening the conversation hoping for good news, "Did you find Jimmy?" "Well Mr. Shannon, yes and no, we . . . ." "What do you mean, yes and no?" Eileen asked. Mr. Blackstone, Mr. Hanney and the sheriff sat quietly, they decided to let Dale do the explaining. "Mr. and Mrs. Shannon, I don't mean to be rude, but if you will just listen till I'm finished, I will explain everything, I also have some pictures to show you and I took notes on what we found." They both agreed to listen while Dale did his explaining. Opening the envelope, he took the out the pictures then opened his note book to the first page before speaking.

"Mr. And Mrs. Shannon, on the first day, Fred and I started up the mountain where I first saw Jimmy's foot prints, now keep in mind those mountains sides are steep, about half way up, we saw where he slipped and slid down five or six feet," (He showed them picture number one) referring to his notes, he continued, "The sun doesn't shine through the trees so the pine needles were still wet from all the rain these past three weeks, we found more foot prints near the top," (He showed them picture two), "Then we found where he spent the night," (Showed them picture three of the small cave.)

From the cave, we followed his trail along the mountain top till it started down, from there we saw a small clearing at the bottom, we figured that is where he went, on the way down we saw where he slipped two more times," (Handing them pictures four and five) "In the clearing, there is a small creek, we found more foot prints along both banks, some broken grass and weeds," (Pictures six, seven, eight and nine) "He drank from the creek then headed south, we think he was looking for some wild vegetables, they are known to grow along creek and river banks.

"We spent the first night in the clearing by the creek. The second day we started following his trail south, but we lost it, the grass and weeds where he walked was standing upright, we did see animal tracks, but no foot prints, there was no sign, since we knew he was going south, that's the way we went. When we were on the south side of the clearing, we started up the next mountain we picked up his trail again when we saw where he slipped." (Pictures ten, eleven and twelve).

"He made his way down the mountain to where it wasn't so steep, there was another small clearing, we found foot prints of three people, Jimmy's and two others, a man and a woman." "WHAT," Eileen gasped, "You mean a man and a woman saw him?" "Whom?" She asked. "I did not say they saw him, and I do not know who they are!" "But didn't they leave any sign, foot prints, anything?" "Mrs. Shannon, may I continue?" Dale asked. "Sorry," she said. He showed them pictures thirteen and fourteen, one was foot prints of two people walking side by side, the other footprints are Jimmy's. "There were also some tire tracks from the tread I would say a four wheel drive vehicle." He showed them number fifteen. "How in the world did a vehicle get up there?" Frank asked.

"Don't know, we didn't follow the tracks, we do know the man and woman left the vehicle and went toward the mountain, Jimmy's foot prints were in front of where they parked, then he laid on the ground and crawled backward a way's" Dale told them, (Pictures sixteen, seventeen). When he got on his feet, he walked backward to the trees before turning and walking away, soon he started running, he ran a long way before he stopped to rest. We found where he rested, that is where we stayed the second night."

Turning the page in his note book, Dale continued, "The third day we crossed the clearing and followed his trail up another mountain until we lost it, we looked for over an hour before we found it again, he was still heading south, on top of the mountain were huge boulders, nothing he could use as shelter," (pictures eighteen nineteen twenty, were of the cluster of boulders, Jimmy's foot prints and mountain scenery,)

"Now Mr. and Mrs. Shannon, I want you to listen very carefully, what I am about to tell you isn't going to be pleasant, it is also the reason I said yes and no when you asked me if we found Jimmy. Before I go on, just let me say that he is very good at being a young mountain man!" "What do you mean a young mountain man, he's not a young mountain man, and he sure as hell don't belong up in those mountains, he belongs here, at home." said Eileen getting more frustrated every minute. "You said you have more news for us, what is it?" Frank asked. With Eileen's abrupt outbursts, Dale wasn't feeling as compassionate as he did when he first got there, so he told them the rest of what they found, in no uncertain terms.

"What we found is this, we left the cluster of boulders going south, the mountain started downhill, following his trail we found a hole in the ground, more like a small wolf den, checking the area, we found cut branches that he used to cover the entrance. From the looks of the area, he spent the night there. We found two empty half pint milk cartons and some clear plastic wrap. We also know that is where the fight began." "What fight?" asked Frank. "And what do you mean milk cartons and plastic wrap, Jimmy didn't take any food with him, that's why we didn't think he left, that he went around back to the patio like he always did."

"Jimmy was in a fight with a bear or a mountain lion, maybe even a wolf," Dale explained." We don't know which it was, some of the foot prints were scuff marks on the ground, we did make out several clear prints of a young bear, at the wolf den is where we first saw the blood!" Dale showed them the rest of the pictures, then, he explained what they were. "In those pictures you can see the wolf den on the side of the mountain, the blood on the ground and rocks, where Jimmy slid down or whatever he was fighting slid down the mountain side, the last picture is of a large pool of blood, we don't know if it is Jimmy's or what animal he was fighting.

Fred took the pictures, I made notes and put samples of the blood in plastic bags, you can see the rock I'm pointing at," Dale was explaining, "It is covered with blood, also you can see a small hand print in blood, We looked the area over for a hundred yards in every direction, we found nothing, no foot prints or skid marks of Jimmy's or of any animal big or small leading downhill, there were no drag marks either, like something was being dragged. His trail ended at that pool of blood, you can see boot prints, paw prints, scuff and scrape marks. Jimmy must have put up one hell of a fight. We never found any remains neither, of Jimmy or of animal. The paw prints in this picture are fresher than the ones in the first picture you saw, they were made after the fight." It was when Dale said 'remains,' Eileen started crying hysterical, she couldn't help it, she couldn't believe her son was killed by a bear, mountain lion or even a wolf, then possibly eaten, or that his body was carried off somewhere, never to be found.

"Mr. and Mrs. Shannon, I'm sorry, I want you to know Fred and I brought the rock with blood on it and the samples back with us, we told

Sheriff Macklin about this and he sent the samples to the lab, to check for DNA, we'll have to wait for the results." It was then that sheriff Macklin spoke, "Mr. and Mrs. Shannon, if you don't mind, I would like to get a sample of your saliva, to send to the lab for testing. The lab will then have something to compare the blood to. Both Frank and Eileen agreed. Sheriff Macklin took two viles from his shirt pocket, with cue tips in them using one on each he capped then labeled the viles. "Mr. and Mrs. Shannon, do you have any questions?" Sheriff asked. "Yes, I do," Eileen said, still crying . . . (sob) "Sher . . . hic . . . sheriff what if all the blood in these pictures are animal blood, and not Jimmy's, what then?"

"Mrs. Shannon, if that's the result of the blood tests, I guess we start looking again, at least we have a starting point, Mr. Haley can take us to where the fight was and we can begin from there, and work our way south." "Sheriff, do you have any reason not to believe that all the blood in these pictures is from animals? Maybe two bears, mountain lions or maybe even wolves got into a fight and one killed the other, isn't that possible?" Frank asked. "NO," said Mr. Haley, "The rock we brought back with blood on it, had a bloody hand print, a small hand, that is why we believe Jimmy had fought the animal, and some of that blood in those pictures is his." "And if what you are saying is true, Mr. Haley, what can we expect?" asked Frank. "Mr. Shannon, if the results of the lab test are what Fred and I think they will be, I would say that your son Jimmy is no longer alive, I'm truly sorry!"

"Mr. And Mrs. Shannon, we will know for sure when the lab tests results come back, that will take three or four weeks, maybe longer, till then, we can only wait, when the results come back, I will come by and let you read it." Said sheriff Macklin. The five men got up, Frank went to the front door with them to say goodbye, they all shook hands, Eileen remained seated at the kitchen table crying. She was looking at the pictures, when Frank returned, he sat next to her, "OOH Frank!" she cried, "Jimmy can't be dead, he, just can't." "We don't know that hon." He said, "We'll just have to wait!" Jodie had come down stairs when she heard the front door shut, standing just inside the kitchen, she heard what her mother said and she too started crying, yelling as loud as she could, she yelled, "NO, NO, NO, Jimmy can't be dead, he isn't dead, I love him, why doesn't he come home?" She sat on the floor, covering her face with her hands she started shaking, sobbing uncontrollably.

Frank went to her, picking her up, he tried to comfort her, still crying, she started to squirm, pushing herself away from her dad. "I want down!" she said, when Frank put her down, she looked up at him, with tears running down her face, "You don't love me, and you don't love Jimmy, if you did, you wouldn't let him go, and you wouldn't be so mean to us, I hate you!" Jodie turned and ran upstairs, in her room she slammed the door and locked it. Eileen hurried upstairs after her, finding the door locked, she knocked . . . "Jodie, open the door." No answer, Knock, Knock, "Jodie, open this door!" "Go away, I hate you!" Jodie screamed. Eileen kept trying, but there was no response.

Eileen went down stairs to the kitchen, Frank was looking at the pictures, when she sat down, Frank said, "I heard, She'll calm down, right now she's just upset, but we will have to try to explain this to her!" "SHE'S UPSET," Eileen said in a loud voice, "WHAT THE HELL AM I? I DON'T LIKE LOOKING AT THESE PICTURES KNOWING JIMMY COULD BE DEAD AND EATEN BY SOME WILD ANIMAL. GET RID OF THEM." "Eileen, you have to calm down, I don't like these pictures either, and I sure as hell don't like what they are reveling, but you know as well as I you aren't doing yourself, or Jodie any good acting this way, we both have to stay calm, for her sake as well as our own, besides we don't know that Jimmy's . . . . gone, ... we'll just have to wait for the lab results."

The next morning Jodie went down stairs in her jammies, she sat in her usual chair at the table. Frank was in his chair drinking coffee Eileen was at the stove fixing breakfast. "Good morning sweetie." she said. Jodie didn't answer, she just sat there, her face had a sad look, her eyes were red from crying most of the night, and her face was dirty, smeared with the tears she had shed and wiped away. She just sat there like a stone statue, not looking at either of her parents. Eileen had fixed a good breakfast of bacon, eggs and hash brown potatoes, with orange juice and toast. She put all three plates on the table, then sat down, she and Frank started eating, but Jodie did not, she couldn't, she looked at where Jimmy sat and the chair was empty, he was gone, maybe dead, never to come home again.

"Jodie you have to eat, it isn't good for you if you don't," Eileen said. Jodie didn't say anything or did she try to eat, she just sat there, "Frank, what are we going to do? she hasn't eaten anything since noon yesterday, it has to be the news we heard the about Jimmy." "I don't know, Eileen, we can't force her to eat. She will eat when she gets hungry enough!" "I should take her to the doctor, he can examine her, make sure she okay."

When breakfast was over, Frank and Eileen cleared the table and washed the dishes, Jodie still just sat there, not moving. When everything was done, Eileen looked at Jodie, "Jodie what's . . . ." Without a word and without looking at them, Jodie got up from the table, with her head bowed low she walked slowly upstairs to her room, closed and locked the door. When she was leaving the kitchen, both Frank and Eileen could see the tear drops fall from her face, but she made not a sound, not a whimper.

Chapter Eleven

It was a quiet peaceful night, when Jimmy woke up, the sun was shining, sitting up he stretched and yawned. Bear also had awakened, sitting there looking up at Jimmy, he whined. Reaching in the basket he got the two hind legs of the rabbit, using the rock floor, he sliced the meat into strips, cutting bears into smaller pieces, and they both ate. Bear let out a low growl, as he ate. After eating and still naked, Jimmy strapped the bowie knife around his right leg, he didn't bother putting on his close, 'Why should I, 'He thought, 'I'm the only one up here in these mountains!' picking up bear, he slowly made his way under the water fall, across the pond to the north bank.

Looking around to make sure it was safe, not seeing any other animal near nor far, he put bear down so he could run and play. Going over to the willow tree where he had left the wood branches for his bow and arrows, he sat down on the soft green grass. Using his knife, he peeled away the bark then trimmed around where the smaller branches were, making the stick he would use as his bow and staff, nice and smooth, then he made a notch three inches from the end at both ends. Holding it out, looking at it, he knew it would be a good bow, it was four feet long and thick, it would take a lot of bending before it broke. He laid it aside, picking up one of the sticks for an arrow, he heard bear growling, standing up quickly, he looked for bear, not seeing him, he heard bear growl again, it was coming from where he had re-made the rabbit snare.

Hurrying over, he saw bear snarling and growling at a dead rabbit that had gotten caught in the snare, when the rabbit got caught it tried to get free, he tried to run then jumping, trying to run pulled against the string, the slip knot just got tighter and tighter till the rabbit choked himself to death. Taking the string from the rabbit's neck he reset the snare then he took the rabbit away from the pond before he cleaned it and removed the skin, he kept the skin, just as he had the other one, he didn't know what he would use them for but was sure they would come in handy. Heading back to the creek, he washed the blood off the rabbit and his hands, thinking that it got caught sometime last night. Being dead for a short time the meat would be good because the cold night air would preserve it.

With some string, Jimmy tied the rabbit to a willow branch then he got busy making his arrows, peeling the bark off and scrapping the wood smooth, he made a groove at one end of each, cutting the feathers he found in half, length ways, he measured each one then cut them the same length, he then doubled the string and cut a piece into two-one foot lengths, unraveling the strings into three pieces, one foot long, he tried to tie three feathers at the notched end of one of the arrows at the same time, having difficulty, he decided to tie two feathers instead, that was easier. The feathers tied on, having no arrow heads, he sharpened the end into a sharp point, with the arrows done. Jimmy took the string and doubled it longer than the bow. Then he tied the ends of the string into a knot, tying one end of the string at the notch at one end of the bow.

Standing, he placed his left leg in between the wood and string, using the ground and his leg as leverage, he bent the bow into an arc, pulling the string tight around the other notch, he made another adjustment by bending the bow just a little more, satisfied, he held the string tight with his thumb and forefinger, releasing the tension he then twisted the string till the two strands became one. Using a little more string past his measurement he made a small loop tied a nonslip knot. He cut the string, then bent the bow and slipped the small loop over the end into the notch.

He picked up one of the arrows, placed the notch on the string, looking around for bear he wanted to make sure he was safe, bear was at the creek drinking water, Jimmy, facing away from bear, he raised the bow and pointed the arrow into the air, he pulled the arrow back with his fingertips, the way his father had showed him and noticed how hard he had to pull, straining, he pulled till he couldn't pull anymore, he let the arrow fly, It sailed upward, going and going till it looked like a little speck in the sky, then started down, it seemed to be coming straight down, it stuck in the ground about eighty feet from Jimmy. "WOW," he thought,

'This works great'. When he was walking to get the arrow, he felt a pain in his right hand, looking at his bandaged hand he saw blood coming from under the bandage, he unwrapped his hand he saw that the cut had reopened.

'Dang', he thought, 'I did this when I strained pulling the bow back.' Retrieving the arrow, he went to the creek to wash his hands and bandage it again. He decided not to practice shooting the arrows till his hand healed instead he would spend the next two days making a quiver for his arrows. When he was finished, he put the arrows in it then put it over his shoulder to see how it fit. The feather end of the arrows came up about six inches above the quiver and just above his right shoulder. It took him a couple hours to make the quiver, in the meantime bear had come to his side, laid down and was asleep, looking around he saw a deer come out of the trees on the other side of the clearing, it walked a few steps, stopped, bent her head down for a bite of grass, the deer was walking on an angle toward the creek and toward him. Jimmy noticed the sun was low in the sky, it was late afternoon and the shadows were getting long, and soon it would be dark, he paid no attention to the deer, gathering up his bow and quiver of arrows, he picked up bear and headed for the cave.

Joseph Blackstone, Dale Haley, and Fred Hanney went back to the reservation. Joseph called for a Council meeting for that evening. At the meeting he explained to the Council the findings of Dale and Fred. "The sheriff said it will take three or four weeks before we get the results," Joseph was saying, "He said he will call me and let me know what the results are. I have a feeling the Shannon family will want our help again. I am asking the Council, what should we do? Do you believe we should help them again, or not?" The members of the Council mumbled and quietly whispered among themselves till a decision was reached.

Mr. Jack Spencer (Falling White Star) the eldest member spoke, "We have come to a decision, It is clear what Mr. Haley and Mr. Hanney has found, they did a good job following the boy's trail till the trail ended in a pool of blood, we will wait for the sheriff to tell us what the lab report says. Then the council will meet again, but keep in mind, there is a young boy, a ten year old, all alone up in those mountains, if he hasn't been killed by which ever wild animal he fought. If, and I emphasize IF, If the boy is still alive, he is a brave young warrior, and we should help the Shannon family if they ask for our help."

"It is true what you say Jack," Said Joseph, "The Council's decision stands, we will wait to hear from the sheriff, and see if the Shannon family asks for our help. If they do, we will help them." When the meeting was over, Joseph asked, "Jack, can you stay? I would like to talk to you!" As the other council members were leaving, Jack Spencer stayed seated. Joseph sat in a chair near him. "Jack, you know as much as I do about the Shannon boy, what is your personal opinion on him surviving a fight with a wild animal?" "Well Joe, you know as well as I, that a young boy who has never lived in the mountains, or has never been taught how to survive or to read sign, doesn't stand a chance. As far as fighting a wild bear, mountain lion or even a wolf, I would say he lost. I believe the boy is dead."

"You believe the boy is dead, and you still want to help the Shannon's if they ask?" "Yes Joe, I do, I think they should know for sure if their son is alive or dead. The lab report may tell us, if all the blood samples are animal, then it is possible the boy is still alive, we must look for him." "Thanks Jack, that's how I feel, I will choose four men at the next council meeting, if as you say all the blood samples are animal, but I don't think they are, don't forget the hand print in blood on the rock, Jimmy may have won the fight, but he may be wounded and is hiding somewhere!" "Yes Joseph, that's possible, if he is wounded and hiding, he will die from his wound, we won't hear from the sheriff for weeks, by then it could be too late!"

When Jimmy woke up the next morning, it was just breaking day, looking toward the water falls he could tell it was getting light, but it was still darker than usual, going to the water he looked out and saw the sky covered with dark clouds, and the air also felt colder. 'Well it looks like rain again,' he thought, 'It's also colder. I wonder what day and month this is.' Going back to his bed, he gathered up his clothes, not wanting to get them wet, he decided to put them on after he crossed the pond. Putting the quiver on his back, he picked up his bow, and bear, made his way under the falls and across the pond, on the north bank he put everything down then started getting dressed, he was just pulling his pants up when he saw a few snowflakes.

'SNOW', he thought as he was looking around, 'It's too early to snow, it's only July or is it. I don't even know what day or month it is.' That got him thinking, he pulled his pants up then sat down beside bear, 'Let's see,' while petting bear, 'I left home the day before my birthday that was the afternoon of the third, I climbed the mountain and stayed in a small cave, that's where I found bear, a lot of days and nights have passed, maybe even weeks. I'm up here all alone, why should I worry about what day or month it is.' Bear was looking up at him, he growled.

Jimmy got up and untied the other half of the rabbit from the branch where he had tied it the evening before, the rabbit was stiff from the cold weather, but not frozen, he managed to cut it into strips, he and bear ate, he still hated the taste of raw meat, the snow was coming down more plentiful in big flakes. 'I have to figure out how to build a fire and get us some more meat.' Fully dressed, he put his coat on, put the quiver on his back, picked up his bow, going to the creek he unwrapped his hand, the cut wasn't bleeding but it was a dark red all around the cut, he put his hand in the cold water and held it there for a few minutes.

Using the second strip of blanket he rewrapped his hand, rinsed the one he took off and hung it over a branch to dry, It was still early morning and the snow was coming down harder. 'I don't have time to figure out how long I have been gone, I need to get some wood and try to start a fire, It's going to get colder and I have to find something to eat.' Picking up his bow he looked at bear, holding his right hand out with palm down, motioning for bear to stay.

With bow in hand he started across the clearing looking for wood, it wasn't long till he found a fallen dead tree, putting his bow over his back, he piled smaller stick in his arms, holding as many as he can, he started back to the cave when he saw movement across the creek, he froze, standing still he slowly turned his head and saw it was a small deer. Looking at it, he didn't see any white spots and it wasn't orange color, it was sort of greyish brown so he knew it wasn't a fawn. His first thought was 'meat' as slow as he could he squatted down, laying the wood on the ground he slowly removed his bow keeping an eye on the deer, he tried to string it but from a squatting position it was hard to do.

Still squatting he put his left foot between the wood and string, he slowly stood, using his leg as leverage he bent the bow into an arc as he slid the string up to the notch, removing his leg, the deer saw him and ran several yards then stopped, looking back, the deer saw little movement but felt no danger, notching an arrow, he guessed the distance to be about sixty five yards, raising his bow and aiming, he pulled the arrow back, just then the deer took off running. This situation reminded him of a program he saw on some sports channel that said, when deer hunting, and the deer starts to run, you should aim just ahead and above the deer, the arc the arrow will travel, will be enough to cover the distance so that the deer and arrow meet at the same junction at the same time.

Taking careful aim, he raised the bow and arrow, he aimed about thirty feet in front of the deer, and fifteen feet above it, letting the arrow fly, he watched it, it arced upward at great speed, angling down, the arrow and deer met, the arrow penetrated the deer's neck, as it fell, Jimmy took off running, he didn't want it to get away, he splashed a crossed the creek and pulled out his knife on the run, reaching the deer just as it was getting up, he jumped on the deer's back, he wrapped his left arm around its neck the best he could, and his legs around its stomach and squeezed, then he stabbed it and kept stabbing it until it fell. The deer did try to run and jump, he turned quickly trying to throw Jimmy off.

When the deer fell, Jimmy fell with it, he held on with all his might till the deer stopped kicking, lying there, he was out of breath and breathing hard, waiting and trying to catch his breath, looking up at the sky, the clouds were mostly dark and the wind was blowing, he heard some thunder and saw some lightning but it was a long way off to the southwest, the way he wanted to go. It was midmorning and it felt like it was getting colder, not warmer, the snow was still falling and started to cover the ground. The deer wasn't moving, so he knew it was dead.

Pulling his arm and leg out from underneath, he stood up and looked around hoping there were no other animals in the clearing, he didn't see any, what he did see was how much more beautiful the clearing was becoming, the green of the pine trees, the yellows, reds, and gold colors of leaves of the oak, maple and aspen all covered with a dusting of snow. 'I hope it don't snow to much' he thought, 'If it does . . . it will be hard walking and more slippery, I must be pretty high up, it don't snow in July or August, when I leave, I will get off the top of this mountain and out of the snow.'

He had work to do, he pulled the arrow from the deer's neck and put it back in the quiver, with his knife he cut open the deer's belly and removed the all the insides, satisfied, he put the bow over his back took hold of both hind legs and dragged the deer toward the cave. The deer was just a small yearling, but it was still a hard struggle to drag it, he decided to cut off the hind quarters and leave the rest for the other animals. But first he would skin the whole deer, he could use the skin.

The skin and two hind quarters would be easy to carry. Inside the cave he dropped the meat away from where he and bear slept, that done, he went out to get bear, he found bear by a willow tree, curled up and shivering, he picked him up and put him inside his coat so he would get warm, it has been more than a month now since he found bear in that small cave on that first night he left home and bear was getting bigger, it won't be too long before he'll be too big to carry.

Petting and rubbing bear to help warm him, Jimmy looked around to see how deep the snow was getting, across the clearing by the dead fallen tree where he was when he first saw the deer, he saw a lone grey and white wolf walking toward him, he tried to get his bow off his back with one hand, and still hold onto bear inside his coat with the other. Seeing the wolf, which was still a ways off, his thoughts were running wild, 'I hope I don't have to fight that wolf, I wish I had a gun, I wish that wolf would go away, I can't fight that wolf with bear inside my coat, he'll fall out the bottom, I don't want that wolf to see me go into the cave, he'll know where we are, I guess I have no choice but to fight.'

With his bow in his right hand, he switched it to his left then took bear out of his coat, putting him on the ground, he took an arrow from the quiver and notched it on the string and waited to see what the wolf was going to do. He knew that animals could smell blood a long ways away, standing there he waited, his shoes, sox and pants were wet from wading across the pond, he started shivering, the air was cold and with the wind blowing made it seem even colder.

Keeping a close eye on the wolf, he looked down to see if bear was okay, bear had walked over to the willow tree and was lying down, he too was shivering. 'I have to get us down off this mountain where it is warmer,' he thought, the wolf had stopped, with his nose in the air, he could smell the deer blood, he turned, crossed the creek and headed toward the smell. Jimmy kept watching, maybe the wolf would come back, but he didn't, after eating, the wolf ran back into trees on the other side of the clearing and disappeared. With the danger gone, Jimmy picked up bear and the blanket bandage from the branch and went into the cave, which was a lot warmer than outside. Next he gathered as much dry wood as he could along with some dry grass hoping he can start a fire.

Inside the cave, with bear covered up in the blanket, Jimmy found a good spot for a fire, it was level with rocks near, getting more rocks he made a small ring, it wasn't too close to his bed, but close enough to keep them warm. After putting some dry grass and sticks in the ring, he sat thinking about a program he saw on TV about how to start a fire using sticks, with one stick lying flat and another upright, using a third stick with a string wrapped around the upright stick several times and tied at both ends like a bow, then with some grass or paper on the flat stick at the junction, using a flat rock to hold the upright stick in place, see-saw the upright stick back and forth to create friction and get the sticks hot enough to start a fire.

Thinking of this he followed the directions he remembered, see-sawing back and forth as fast as he could, he soon saw a little smoke, with his arm and shoulder getting tired he knew he couldn't stop, he had to have a fire, as it was, he was freezing, his pants, shoes and sox were still wet, he had to get them off. If he gets a fire going it will warm the cave even more.

The little smoke he saw became more and more, he see-sawed faster, his arm and shoulder felt like they were burning but he couldn't stop, not now, then like magic, a small flame appeared, it caught the dry grass on fire and the flame grew bigger, as fast as he could he picked up the burning stick and grass and put in the ring with the other grass and sticks, soon he had a nice little fire going, adding more sticks the fire grew, he never thought about ventilation, but it didn't seem to matter, the smoke drifted to the rear of the cave and disappeared. There must be some kind of small hole back there, he didn't know, but it wasn't big enough to create a big draft, or maybe the water fall blocked most of the draft. Ten minutes later the cave was nice and warm, he added more sticks to keep the fire going, looking at the pile of sticks, he knew it wouldn't last the rest of the day and all night, he had to get more.

Wading across the pond several more times didn't appeal to him, but he knew had to do it, outside on the north bank he searched most of the clearing, looking for any kind of wild animal, he saw none, it was still snowing and was about an inch deep. With everything that has happened this morning he guest it to be around noon maybe a little later, the sky was still dark and everything was covered in white. Jimmy made ten trips in and out of the cave gathering wood, each time he carried as much as he could, he didn't want to go out again. He wanted to stay in where it was warm. Entering the cave on his tenth trip he saw bear at the deer meat chewing on it, Jimmy laughed out loud.

The cave being nice and warm, Jimmy undressed, he took off all his close and hung them over some rocks to dry, after adding a few more sticks to the fire he got his knife, he put bear back on the blanket then started cutting off a big slice of meat, cutting that into smaller pieces, all the while he was thinking, 'I don't have to eat raw meat anymore, now I can cook the meat.'

Placing the strips of meat over a stick, he held it over the fire, in a short time the meat started cooking, when he tried to turn it over the meat fell into the fire. Fishing the meat out of the fire, he went to the water fall to wash them off, "Think dummy," he said to himself, "you have to cut notches in the meat then put the stick through the notches, having done this he once again held the meat over the fire, this time the stick caught on fire behind the meat and the weight broke the stick, and into the fire went the meat. After fishing the meat out again, he looked at bear, bear was just sitting there with his head tilted to one side, "Well bear," he said, "Looks like we have to eat the meat raw again," after eating Jimmy went to the entrance, with one of the water bottles he reached out for water and filled it, sloshing the water around in his mouth then spitting it out, he did this several times. Cutting up the deer into several large chunks he piled the meat on the highest rock he could find. Then he scraped the hide clean, folded it and put it up to. With all his work done, he washed his hands then he settled down on the blanket with bear, being warm and their bellies full they were content, they both laid down and covered up, soon they were both sound asleep.

Jimmy woke up shivering during the night, the fire had died down to ambers, he blew lightly into the ashes and saw a red glow, there were still some hot ambers, hurrying he got some dry grass and sticks, placing them on the ambers, he blew gently again, just enough to turn the ambers red, shivering he kept blowing till the red ambers caught the dry grass and sticks on fire. With the fire going again, he put on more sticks, still shivering he hurried under the blanket to warm up, he would stay awake and feed the fire till it was warm in the cave, but as the cave grew warmer he fell asleep before adding more wood.

Jimmy was still sleeping when bear woke up, it was daylight and he was hungry, licking Jimmy's face, he growled and whined till Jimmy woke up. Opening his eyes, Jimmy laid there a few minutes, bear was still whining, "Okay Bear," he said, "Your, hungry, me to." Jimmy got up, put more wood on the fire which had burned down to coals again, it wasn't as cold now as it was before, he put a little dry grass and wood on the fire. There was only a trace, but enough to catch the grass and the sticks on fire. He cut some strips off the deer, this time he didn't try to cook them, he and bear ate the meat raw, while they were eating Jimmy thought it was time to get down off this mountain.

After he ate, he got dressed, then went to the water fall, he filled all four bottles with water, he rinsed his mouth, he hated the taste of deer blood, looking out he saw that the sky was partly cloudy, the sun shone, and the brightness reflecting off the snow made him squint, but most of all it wasn't snowing. Now is the time he thought, returning to his bed, he started gathering up the things he would take, he knew he couldn't take it all, but he was going to take as much as he could. He would carry as much meat as he can. By noon he had accomplished what he wanted to do.

He placed the bottles on top of the blanket, he stretched out the deer hide then placed the two hind quarters on it, cutting two strips of bear hide he used them to sew the hide into a pouch he could carry on his back. The rest of the deer he would take outside so the other animals would have something to eat. He didn't relish crossing the pond several times but there was no other way out that he knew of.

Everything was ready, he was just about to take the rest of the deer outside when he got an idea, 'The rabbit hides, I can use the rabbit hides to keep my feet warm, after I get everything out, I can take off my shoes and sox, make sox out of rabbit hide, with the fur side in, it will keep my feet warm and not let in the water or cold from walking in the snow.' An hour later, he was ready to go. With the pouch of deer meat on his back, he put the arrow quiver over his shoulder and on his left side, he put bear inside his coat on the right side, tied the twine tight around his waist so bear wouldn't fall out, picking up his bow and the basket, he headed south.

Chapter Twelve

Four weeks later, Sheriff Macklin received an envelope with a copy of the lab report, he was hesitant to open it, he had a bad feeling about what the report would say. Slowly, he did open it and pulled out two sheets of paper, he read the report carefully. He wanted to make sure he knew exactly what it said. The more he read, the more his face grew grimmer, when he finished, he laid the papers down, leaned back in his chair and said out loud, "Jimmy's dead, this report proves it."

What the lab report says . . . that the bagged samples and the blood on the rock are both human and animal. The animal blood is most likely bear or wolf, the blood hand print on the rock is human, there was a mixture of human and animal blood in the bagged samples that were submitted, with the saliva samples of Mr. and Mrs. Shannon, the DNA, of the human blood on the rock, and what was found in the bagged samples was a very close MATCH to the saliva samples of Mr. and Mrs. Shannon.

In the box marked 'deceased' was the name, JAMES LEE SHANNON, at the bottom of the second page was a space marked 'REMARKS' in this space was typed. 'The results of all the blood samples submitted are as follows. The blood in the plastic bags and on the rock, were found to be human and animal. The animal blood tested proved to be either bear or wolf. The RH factor of the animal blood is 'AN Negative,' the RH factor of the human blood tested is 'AB Negative,' the RH factor of the saliva samples of Mr. and Mrs. Shannon is 'AB Negative,' The DNA of both samples is a MATCH. From these results, and from the pictures submitted, with the amount of blood shone and for the reason for these tests, I can only surmise that the son of Mr. and Mrs. Frank Shannon, JAMES LEE SHANNON is no longer alive.

Of course there was the usual information, date the samples were received, date the tests were performed, and who performed the tests, who they were submitted by, and why they were submitted. etc. Sheriff Macklin had some phone calls to make, and he had to go to the Shannon resident to break the news and let them read the report for themselves. He had promised this. The first call was to chief Middlestone. After dialing, Joseph picked up on the second ring, "Hello." "Mr. Middlestone, this is Sheriff Macklin, I'm calling to inform you that I have the lab report, and it isn't good. It says that after the test were done, there conclusion is that Jimmy is no longer alive."

"I was afraid of that! does it say what animal the blood belonged to?" "Yes it does, it says a bear or wolf, have you talked with the Shannon's lately?" "No sheriff, the Council and I were waiting for your call. I will tell the council about the report, are you going to inform the Shannon's and show them the report?" Asked Joseph. "Yes, I am, I told them they could read it!" "This is a sad day sheriff, I don't envy you, but it has to be done." "Yes Joseph, it does!"

Next, Sheriff Macklin called the warehouse where Frank worked and talked to Mr. Norton, he told him about the lab report, and asked him not to say anything to Frank, that he was going to call on them this evening and let them read the report. "Sheriff, this is very sad, I'm so sorry," Mr. Norton was saying," I won't tell anyone, Frank will probably take a few days off to console his family." "I'm sure he will I only wish I had better news." Sheriff Macklin said. "Yes sheriff, I bet you do, this is just horrible. It's a terrible way to die they won't even be able to bury his body, how sad!" "Yes Mr. Norton, it is sad, thanks for helping me on this." "Not a problem Sheriff, if there's anything else I can do, just let me know." "Thanks Mr. Norton."

Sheriff Macklin made a copy of the lab report and put in the Shannon file along with their missing person report. Next he went to the outer office where some deputies and civilian workers were. "May I have every ones attention," he said in a loud voice, everyone stopped what they were doing and looked at him. "You all know about the Jimmy Shannon case. That we were waiting for the lab results, (He held up the two sheets paper) these two sheets of paper are the results.

What they say is that the blood samples submitted, were both human and animal, the animal blood tested . . . , is either bear . . . , or wolf. At this point the Sheriff started to choke up. The human blood . . . . and the saliva . . . , (He had tears in his eyes at this point, and every so often he would pause) samples of Mr. and Mrs. Shannon are a . . . Match. In the box marked deceased is the name . . . JAMES LEE SHANNON. The final result is that Jimmy is no longer . . . alive. Dispatcher, please radio all units and inform them. I'm sure after this there won't be anyone looking for him and there certainly will be no more search parties.

The Sheriff then quickly turned and went into his office he didn't want the others to see him cry. He sat in his chair with a handkerchief in his hand and cried, thinking, 'That is a horrible way to die, to be in a fight with a wild bear or wolf and be torn apart, trying his best to win the fight and stay alive. A ten year old boy wouldn't stand a chance.' He sat there for a long time, contemplating about the events that must have happened, leading up to and including the fight Jimmy had fought. He couldn't visualize any of it.

At five pm that evening the Sheriff called the Shannon resident, Frank answered, "Hello." "Mr. Shannon, this is Sheriff Macklin, I'm calling to let you know I have the lab results, would it be alright to come over about eight this evening?" Frank hearing this, started shaking, the tone of the sheriff's voice was saying bad news. "Yes . . . , Sheriff, eight will be . . . fine!" "Thanks Mr. Shannon, see you then." When Frank hung up, he just stood there, staring into space, his mind went blank, it wasn't until Eileen called his name that his mind functioned again.

Eileen was standing by the stove fixing dinner when she said, "FRANK . . . FRANK, what's the matter? Are you alright? your white as a sheet!" Jodie had finally started talking to her parents after they explained about Jimmy. That they didn't really know anything yet, as far as they knew he was still alive. Jodie was seated at the table, Frank looked at Eileen, she could tell he was worried, "That was Sheriff Macklin, he said he has the lab report, he'll be here at eight."

Seeing the worried look on Frank's face, she too started to worry, she didn't want to ask any questions in front of Jodie, but she was dying to know what the sheriff said and what Frank was thinking. He had turned white as a sheet while talking to the sheriff she could only guess that it was bad news. Dinner was ready, the three of them were seated at the table, no one said a word, they didn't even look at each other, Jodie, although she was only six had made up her mind, when the sheriff gets here, her parents were going to tell her to go to her room, that they would explain about Jimmy later, but she wasn't going to do it, she was staying here, she wanted to know about Jimmy too. The only way she would go to her room is if she was carried.

At eight pm, the sheriff, Mr. Middlestone and Mr. Haley arrived, the Sheriff rang the doorbell, Frank opened the door and turned on the porch light, "Gentlemen, come in please." After they entered, Frank closed the door. "We can talk in the kitchen, Eileen is making coffee!" Frank led the way, but he did notice the manila envelope Sheriff Macklin was carrying, Eileen was pouring water into the coffee maker, Jodie was seated where she always sat. "Please sit down gentlemen!" Frank suggested, "Eileen will be done momentarily!" "Good evening gentlemen," Eileen said while still pouring the water, now she started getting nervous, she knew that in a few minutes she would know what the lab report says.

When everyone was seated at the table, Eileen said, "Jodie, I think you better go up . . ." Jodie spoke up, "No, I want to stay here I want to know about Jimmy." Before an argument started between them like last time, sheriff macklin said, "Mr., Mrs. Shannon, I have the lab report, and as I promised, you may read it, then if you wish, we can discuss it and try to answer any questions you may have. Would that be alright?" Frank and Eileen both nodded their heads. The Sheriff then handed Eileen the manila envelope. They both stared at it Eileen then opened it and took out both sheets of paper.

She placed both papers between them and they began to read. When Eileen read Jimmy's name in the box marked deceased, she let out a scream, "NO, NO, . . . this can't be right, Jimmy can't be dead." she started crying, her hands started shaking. "He just can't be!" Frank to started crying, Jodie seeing her parents crying, and what her mother said, made her cry, "Jimmy's dead?" she asked between sobs. "Does that paper say Jimmy's dead?" Jodie asked. Dale Haley then said, "I'm very sorry Mr. And Mrs. Shannon, I truly am. The lab explains their findings on the next page under remarks."

Eileen's hands were shaking so bad she couldn't turn the page so Frank did it for her, they both read the remarks. When Eileen read the last few words, James Lee Shannon is no longer alive. She screamed, "JIMMY . . . JIMMY, I'M SO SORRY, YOU CAN'T BE DEAD, CAN YOU EVER FORGIVE ME? I'M SORRY . . . , I'M SO VERY

SORRY!" crying even harder now, since she heard her mother, Jodie knew Jimmy was dead, she got off her chair, and screamed at them, "I . . . I hate you, y,y, you killed Jimmy. I don't ever want to t . . . , talk to you again, I hate you." she turned and ran upstairs, slamming the door, she locked it, jumped on her bed and cried "Jimmy, why did you have to go, you know I love you and need you, who will protect me now?"

Chapter Thirteen

For the past four weeks Jimmy worked his way south, climbing up and down mountains, across valleys and clearings, stopped at creeks, and small river, if the water was clear he would fill the four small water bottles. The weather was good, the clouds had gone and the sun shined warmer, at least once a week when he was at a river or creek he would strip off his clothes, wash them the best he could then himself. Putting on clean clothes from his backpack, he would lay the clothes he washed over rocks or hang them on bushes or over tree limbs.

Also during the past four weeks, he didn't try using his bow and arrows, the cut on his hand was healing, but it was still red, and it still hurt, not knowing if it was infected or not. For food he set his snare, some days he would catch a rabbit, but most days he didn't. He and bear would go hungry, three, sometimes four days with nothing to eat. This one particular morning, he and bear came down off a mountain side into a large clearing, he hoped there was water, or even a creek of some kind, not seeing any, he made a snare, maybe he could catch a rabbit today, after setting the snare with some greenery for bait, he and bear went over to a nearby pine tree and sat down, with bear on his lap petting him, he watched the snare.

This is the fourth day in which they had nothing to eat, he prayed for a rabbit. While he was sitting there, he looked around, he was always on the look—out for wild animals, not seeing or hearing anything except the breeze whispering through the trees. To keep himself busy he reached over and plucked a lite green leaf off a small plant, it was a couple inches long and slender, he smelled it, there was no oder, he didn't know what it was, he broke it in half to see what was inside, some thick clear slimy liquid slid down his fingers into his palms, he tried to shake it off with no luck, rubbing his hands together trying to get it off he smeared it over both hands and fingers. It was slick, not sticky. 'I'll wash it off at the next creek.' He thought.

With the midmorning sun and a gentle breeze he was getting sleepy, most nights he would wake up at the slightest sound, check to make sure all was well, then have trouble getting back to sleep. The days of traveling south and staying low on the mountain sides as much as possible, he left the snow far behind. He just couldn't keep his eyes open any longer he laid down with bear curled up beside him.

At the Shannon home, sheriff Macklin was saying, "Mr. and Mrs. Shannon, I'm very sorry, is there anything I can do? Do you have any questions?" Mr. Middlestone then said, "I too, am very sorry for your loss! If you wish we can try to find his body?" Frank had finally contained himself, wiped his eyes and blew his nose. Eileen was trying to calm down, still crying, she too wiped her eyes and blew her nose. Frank got up went to the coffee pot and refilled their cups, seated again he said, "Mr. Middlestone, do you really think you can find Jimmy's body? I mean, if he g . . . got into a f, . . . fight with a bear or wolf wo . . . wouldn't it . . . ." he couldn't help it, the thought of his son Jimmy losing a fight with a bear or wolf and his body being torn apart was too much, he started crying again.

For a long time Mr. Middlestone, Mr. Haley, the sheriff and Mr. and Mrs. Shannon sat quietly, no one knew what to say. Eileen was the one who finally spoke up, "Sheriff, how conclusive is this report? Is there a chance it could be wrong? Maybe, Jimmy could still be alive, wounded maybe, but be alive?" "I'm sorry Mrs. Shannon, DNA reports are very conclusive, when they find a match it is one in a billion that it could be wrong." Mr. Haley then asked, "Mrs. Shannon, as Joseph has said, if you want, we will look for your son's body! The chances of finding him are very remote, if he did survive the fight and is wounded, he will look for some place to hide that would make finding him even harder."

"Mr. Haley, do you think a ten year old boy could survive a fight with a bear or wolf?" Eileen asked. "We don't know how the fight went," Dale said, "He might have been able to escape, that mountain side is very steep, anything is possible." It was Frank who spoke next, "Mr. Haley, do you really believe that?" "No sir," said Dale, "I honestly believe your son is . . . gone." "Then why?" Eileen asked, "Why would you want to look for him?" "To do everything we possibly can," Dale said, "To help you in every way to have piece, in your mind and in your heart."

"No Mr. Haley, we thank you for what you did, but no, the only thing we can do now is make arrangements for Jimmy's funeral, we won't be burying him, but at least we can have a memorial service." "Mr., Mrs. Shannon, if you don't mind . . . would it be alright if we attend the service?" asked Joseph. "All of you are more than welcome Mr. Middlestone, but may I ask why?" asked Eileen. "It is for your son!" said Joseph, "Among our people, we believe in honor, just as our forefathers did, to us . . . your son was a brave boy, a brave warrior, he faced and met danger like a man and he should be honored as such."

After the three men left, Frank went back to the kitchen, Eileen was still sitting at the table, she had turned the pictures and the lab report upside down, she didn't want to look at them anymore. Frank poured them both coffee then sat down. "Don't you think we should have asked them to look for Jimmy?" He asked. Eileen was still upset, her stomach was in turmoil, and she was mad. "NO FRANK I DON'T," she said raising her voice, "JIMMY IS DEAD, AND IT'S YOUR FAULT." "Eileen, you don't have to raise your voice, I'm right here, not upstairs, how is it my fault?" "YOUR THE ONE WHO WAS ALWAYS MEAN, OR SHOULD I SAY STRICK TO JIMMY AND JODIE, YOU SAW HOW UPSET SHE WAS, SHE EVEN ASKED YOU WHY WAS YOU WERE SO MEAN TO US, DIDN'T SHE?"

"I wasn't mean, strict maybe I was only trying to teach them, I . . . ." "TEACH THEM WHAT?" "What they needed to learn, and besides you went along with me on what I told them, so your, just as much at fault as I am." "OH NO! YOUR NOT BLAMEING ME, I WENT ALONG WITH YOU ON CERTAIN THINGS IF YOU REMEMBER, I ALSO STUCK UP FOR THE KIDS WHEN YOU WERE WRONG." "Eileen, please don't shout, you need to calm down, we can talk about this without shouting. And yes, I will admit that sometimes I was wrong, but in this, we were both wrong." "What do you mean we were both wrong?" "Aren't you the one who slapped him?" "THAT'S IT FRANK, NOW YOUR BLAMMING ME," she started yelling again, "I'VE HAD IT WITH YOU, YOU AND YOUR MEANESS, YOUR STRICKNESS, YOU'VE CHANGED, YOUR NOT THE SAME MAN I MARRIED, I'LL STAY UNTILL

AFTER THE MEMORIAL SERVICES, THEN JODIE AND I ARE LEAVING, I WANT A DIVORCE, THEN YOU CAN STAY HERE AND GET AS MEAN AND STRICK AT YOURSELF AS YOU WANT."

"WHAT! You want a divorce? Why on earth do you want a divorce? Just because I was strict with Jimmy and Jodie, and I wasn't mean." "That's not the only reason," she had calmed down enough to talk in a normal tone, "Remember before Jimmy was born, you were mean AND strict with me, you even hit me once." She had emphasized the word AND. "Eileen, that's just my nature, that's how I am, you knew that before we were married." "Yeah, well maybe I did, but you have changed, you've gotten meaner and more demanding as the kids got older, I'm not going to put up with it any longer, as I said, I will stay here until after Jimmy's memorial service, and I will be civil, Then Jodie and I are leaving, I have a headache, I'm going to bed."

The next day some of the people in town knew what had happened, Frank and Eileen went to work as usual, Jodie went to school, of course there were the usual condolences from the people they knew. Eileen asked for the next day off so she could make the memorial arrangements, her boss was surprised she had even come in to work today, she told Eileen to take as much time as she needed. Frank called Eileen at work, told her that the newspaper reporter, Mr. Tom Boyle was there and wanted an exclusive, and a picture of Jimmy, he asked her if that would be alright. He didn't want any more trouble or arguments when he got home. Since some of the people already new, she figured it wouldn't take long for the story to spread, so she said okay.

Frank told Mr. Boyle everything, about the search, the pictures, and the lab report remarks. Jimmy's picture and the whole story, was on the front page of the evening newspaper. The service was to be held that Friday from one thirty to three, and the mass from three to three thirty at St. Paul's Catholic Church. On Tuesday before the services Eileen had made the arrangements with the Catholic Church and Watkins funeral parlor. It was to be a closed casket service since Jimmy wasn't there. She would place a recent picture of him on top facing the congregation with flowers on three sides. The reception was to be at the Shannon home right after the service.

She had made these arrangements with the church and Watkins funeral parlor, when talking to Mr. Watkins she asked only for the use of the casket, or to rent it since Jimmy wouldn't be in it. When the service was over he could have it back. Mr. Watkins had read the paper, so he knew the story about Jimmy's death, and told her there will no charge. After that, she made arrangements to buy a plot and a head stone in the local cemetery.

Friday afternoon, Frank, Eileen and Jodie were at the church at noon, the closed casket was in front of the alter, it was a beautiful casket, light silver gray with gold trim, when she saw it, she started crying, the memories of Jimmy, and the memories of how he died hit her hard, in her mind, heart and sole. Jodie had cried on and off ever since they got the news about him. In church, she tried to hold back the tears to no avail, for she too was looking at the casket. It made a mark on her life, her best friend and her protector was gone, she would never see, or talk to him again.

At one, Mr. Middlestone and his family, along with the whole tribal Council and their families were the first ones at the church, they signed the guest register, went in and met with Frank, Eileen and Jodie, with condolences from the tribal Council, they began talking when Mr. Boyle walked in, he too paid his respects, they talked for a while, When others started arriving, the tribal Council and families sat in the first three rows of pews on the right. Between twelve and Twelve thirty, the flower shop delivered fifteen beautiful bouquets of flower arrangements, they were placed all around the casket. By one thirty the church was full, with standing room only. Some of the kids in Jimmy's class were there with their parents.

It was a beautiful service, Father Bishop said a few prayers, a few songs were sung, then he told them what he knew about Jimmy, when he was finished, he asked if anyone would like to come up and say a few words. A few of Jimmy's friends came forth and talked about him, one little girl who liked him very much had tears sliding down her face as she talked about how smart and resourceful he was, how he was always friendly, and willing to help, not only the teacher, but the other students as well.

Mr. Middlestone got up and stood to the right of the casket, "Ladies and gentlemen," he started, "My name is Joseph Middlestone, I am chief of the local Souix tribe, the tribal council and I, and our families, are here to pay tribute and honor Jimmy Lee Shannon, (He held his left hand toward the photo) he was a very brave boy, a brave warrior, he knew the way of the wild . . . he knew the way of mother earth, he understood the wild and dangerous animals of the wild, finally he knew the way of my people, he was a brave warrior, we hold him in our hearts, ... he will be missed."

Eileen got up next to talk about her son she stood by the casket, holding a kleenix in her hand, as she told the story. "Ladies and gentlemen, my son . . . J . . . (sob) Jimmy, was born on the fourth of . . . J . . . July,(sob) at seven ten pm. he was a good boy, like all boy's, from . . . t(sob) time to time, he would get into trouble, nothing serious, just kid stuff. (She blew her nose) When he did something wrong, Frank or I would scold him and he would get mad and say he was leaving home . . . (sniff, sniff) late in the afternoon, this past July 3rd, we scold him for something he didn't do, we didn't know that at the time . . . .

This time, when he said he was leaving home, we thought he would do as he always did, but he didn't, he really left, as all of you probably know, we searched for him for three weeks." By this time Eileen was in full control of her emotions. "Then sheriff Macklin asked Mr. Middlestone and the tribal council to help us look, thanks to Mr. Haley, he saw where Jimmy headed up into the mountains south of town, he and Mr. Hanney set out to look for him.

They followed Jimmy's trail to the end, they found where he spent each night, they took pictures of everything, at the end of Jimmy's trail, there was a lot of blood, also there was foot prints and paw prints along with what looked like scrape marks on the ground and a large pool of blood. They searched the area in all directions for over a hundred yards, they found nothing, no foot prints, or paw prints, or skid marks like something was being dragged. The blood samples and our saliva samples were a match, the only conclusion we have, along with the lab report, is that Jimmy got into a fight with a bear or wolf, and he lost. His body was never found."

At that moment Eileen broke down, she started shaking badly, and she was crying out loud so hard she was unable to catch her breath, try as she might she got to the point where she pasted out. A few people rushed to her to help, she was unresponsive. 9-1-1 was called, most of the congregation stayed seated, when the paramedic's arrived, she was breathing short gasps, they put an oxygen mask over her nose and mouth, placed a back board under her, lifted her onto a gurney, hurried to the ambulance, and rushed her to the hospital.

Father Bishop said "Ladies and gentlemen, we will pray for Mrs. Shannon and her son Jimmy!" Frank and Jodie followed the paramedics out, got to the car and followed the ambulance to the hospital.

Ten minutes later, Frank and Jodie were at the hospital, after parking the car, they entered the emergency entrance and went to the nurses station. "I'm Frank Shannon, my wife was just brought in, she passed out at the Catholic church, can you tell me what room she is in?" "She is in E R Mr. Shannon, the doctor and nurses are with her, won't you please have a seat!" Frank and Jodie sat in the waiting room for what seemed like hours, but it was only forty minutes. During that time, Frank couldn't sit still, he was nervous and worried, Jodie wasn't sure what was happening, she asked, "Daddy, is mommy going to be okay?" Frank wasn't sure what to tell her, so he just said, "I don't know sweetheart I sure hope so!" "Me too!" Jodie said.

Frank saw a doctor come out of one of the emergency rooms and go to the nurses station, they talked a few minutes, then the nurse looked and pointed at Frank, when the doctor came towards him, he stood up. "Mr. Shannon I'm Doctor Paul Mansfield!" "Afternoon doctor Mansfield, my daughter Jodie, how's my wife?" "Mr. Shannon, please come to my office, I need to talk to you!" "My wife Doctor Mansfield, how is she?" "Mr. Shannon, I would rather discuss it in private, not here in the waiting room, please come with me."

Following the doctor through double doors to the right of the waiting room, Frank held Jodie's hand, Doctor Mansfield opened the door to his office, after entering, Doctor Mansfield asked them to have a seat. "Now Doctor Mansfield, will you please tell me how my wife is?" "Mr. Shannon, there is no easy way to say this . . . so I'll just tell you, also I need to ask you some questions . . . Mr. Shannon . . . , your wife passed away she had trouble breathing, when we tried to stabilize her, her heart just stopped, we couldn't get it to start beating again, we did everything we could to save her."

Frank just stared at the doctor, not believing what he just heard, he was speechless, and he felt numb. Jodie on the other hand, understanding what was said, started crying, "My mommy's dead? She was okay little while ago." "I'm very sorry, Jodie," said Doctor Mansfield. Frank picked up Jodie and held her. Tears were sliding down both their faces. "How," Frank asked, "How could this happen, can you tell me that, HOW?"

Chapter Fourteen

Jimmy and bear slept for several hours, when he awoke, he laid very still, listening for any sound, these past two and a half months living in the mountains, and what he has gone through has taught him to be careful, especially the fight he had with a bear. He heard nothing, there was no breeze, none of the tall weeds throughout the clearing were moving, everything was still and quiet. Lying there, he cents something was wrong, but he didn't know what.

Sitting up slowly, he looked all around, he took his time in checking every—thing in the clearing, he didn't see any animal that was as tall, or taller than the weeds. If there was an animal out there he should see it, it would eventually move, so he kept checking, back and forth he moved his head, checking not only the clearing but the wooded area all around the clearing.

Bear was also awake, he woke up when Jimmy sat up, while Jimmy was checking the area, he was also petting bear. It wasn't till bear stood up that the danger presented itself. A rattle snake not twenty feet away, when bear stood the snake reacted, it was coiled ready to strike and started to rattle its tail, Jimmy picked up bear and placed him on his lap, "shhh, shhh," Jimmy whispered, he and bear didn't move, it took a few seconds, but with them not moving the snake settled down then slivered away. With the danger past, Jimmy felt better he got up to check on the snare.

Like the other time, a rabbit got caught with the twine around its neck, fighting to get loose only made it worse, the rabbit died while Jimmy and bear were asleep. After cleaning and skinning the rabbit, and since they both hadn't eaten in almost four days, they ate the whole rabbit, now he had to find some water, he had only a half a bottle left, when they finished eating, Jimmy rinsed his out his mouth, then packed his gear and they headed south. It was midafternoon and wouldn't be getting dark for three or four hours, while on their journey, Jimmy was also looking for a place to spend the night.

Two hours before dark, Jimmy and bear was working their way down a mountain side, he stopped about half way down, looking through the trees, he saw a vast clearing, only a few trees in and around the clearing, the mountains on the other side seemed to be miles away. A little farther down the mountain side is when he first saw them, he stopped, he couldn't believe it, what he saw was some buildings, 'Buildings,' he thought, 'It must be a ranch or a farm.'

Coming out of the trees at the bottom of the mountain, he came to a barb—wire fence, putting the basket over the top, he worked it down by putting his arms between each strand as he lowered it, the basket was now full and heavy, in it was the blanket, rabbit hides, some of the bear and deer skins, plus four small empty plastic water bottles, taking off his backpack he tossed it over, then using his bow/staff for leverage he pushed down the wire making a wider gap to crawl though. They walked across some flat land and up a small rise, at the top they both stopped. "Look bear, it is a ranch," Jimmy said, "Maybe we can get something to eat and drink!"

Standing on the rise he was looking at the back of the ranch house, the corals, pens, and barn were on the right from where he stood. There were a few horses in one of the corals he didn't see any cows in any of the pens or any—where around the ranch house. Looking all around he saw some tiny dots off to his right that might be cows. He and bear started down the rise toward the house, they approached from the left side, not having any more fences to go through, walking to the front with bear beside him, he didn't see or hear any dogs, if there had been, they surely would have attacked bear, or tried to.

At the front, he and bear went up on the porch, he knocked and waited, then knocked again, an elderly man opened the door, when he saw Jimmy he said, "Well my goodness young man, where did you come from?" looking out at the front yard he didn't see a car or any other person, then he noticed bear, "Is that a wolf pup?" he asked. "Yes sir, he is," Jimmy answered. "Sir, we haven't eaten in several days, I was hoping you . . . ." "You haven't eaten in several days, you must be starving son?" the man said. "Yes sir, we are, could you give us something to eat?" The man opened the screen door, "Please, come in."

Jimmy entered the house, but bear hesitated, this was all new and strange to him. "Can bear come in too?" Jimmy asked. "Yes, of course he can, there are no dogs on this ranch." "C'mon bear, it's okay." Bear entered slowly, staying close to Jimmy, they followed the man into the kitchen where his wife was she was at the sink washing dishes. "Edith, we have company, please have a seat young man.

Jimmy sat in the nearest chair at the table, bear stood beside him. "What's your name by the way?" the man asked. "Lee, sir, my name is Lee!" He didn't want to tell them his first name, or his last, so he settled for Lee. "Well Lee, this is my wife Edith, and I am Phillip Adams, this is our ranch, the 'Double Diamond'," Mr. Adams turned to his wife, "Edith, Lee says he and his wolf pup haven't eaten in a few days, do you think we can find something for them?"

"You haven't eaten in a few days," Edith asked, "You must be very hungry, of course we can feed them." She went to the cupboard and got a plate for Jimmy and a bowl for bear, then to the refrigerator and got out some meatloaf, mashed potatoes, gravy, green beans, filled a plate for Jimmy, and the bowl for bear, after putting the plate and bowl in the oven to warm, she got out the bread, butter and silver, glass of water for Jimmy, and a bowl of water for bear.

When the food was placed in front of him and bear, they both ate like there was no tomorrow, they shoveled it in. Mr. and Mrs. Adams sat at the table watching, they couldn't believe that anyone would let a young boy go hungry, they both decided to wait till he was finished before they asked anymore questions. When Jimmy cleaned his plate, he saw that bear was licking the bowl. "Mrs. Adams, could we please have some more?" Jimmy asked. "My goodness Lee, your still hungry?" she asked. "Yes ma'am, bear and I both are."

Waiting patiently for Jimmy to finish eating, Mr. and Mrs. Adams had a lot of questions to ask him. It took him fifteen minutes to finish the second helping, bear was done before him and had drank some water, no longer hungry or thirsty, bear went to Jimmy's side. When Jimmy finally finished, he pushed back from the table and clapped his hands, "Up bear!" he said. Bear jumped up onto his lap, holding and petting him, Jimmy looked at Mr. and Mrs. Adams. "Thank you Mr. and Mrs. Adams for a wonderful dinner, and for bear too." Mrs. Adams responded, "Your more than welcome Lee, you and bear both, how is it you have a wolf pup for a friend, and not a dog?" "I found him in a cave a few months ago, up in the mountains, I found his mother too she had the same markings, only she was dead."

Still petting bear, Jimmy knew they were going to ask him more questions. He would answer them as truthfully as he can, but try not to give too much information as to why he was in the mountains. "Where do you live Lee? I mean, where is your family?" Mr. Adams asked. "I don't have a family sir I do have a sister, what state is this?" "You don't have a family, that's sad, I'm so sorry," said Mrs. Adams, "You don't know what state this is?" "No ma-am, I don't, I don't even know what day or month it is." "Your, kidding, right?" asked Mr. Adams. "No sir, I'm not!" Jimmy replied. "Well Lee, this is south central Wyoming, and today is Sunday, September twenty sixth." Mr. Adams replied. "I didn't see any ranch hands," said Jimmy, "Do you work the ranch by yourselves?" "No Lee, we don't, oh we help out when we can, but we have three ranch hands, three young men who do all the work." Mrs. Adams said. "I didn't see them, are they off today?"

Jimmy was trying to evade their questions by asking questions, it didn't seem to be working. He wanted so much to leave, but he also didn't want to be rude. "I didn't see any cows, do you have cows?" he asked. "Yes, we have cattle, they're out in the pastures, the hands are rounding them up now, bringing them in closer to headquarters, winter isn't far off and we can take better care of them when it snows." said Mr. Adams. "How long does the round up take?" "It'll take them about a week, they left yesterday on horseback. We have a line shack they'll stay in till they round up the cattle, then herd them here." Mr. Adams told him.

"Oh, I see!" Jimmy replied. "Lee, is there anyone we can call, to let them know where you are?" asked Edith. "No ma'am, I only have a sister, she's six." "Who is she staying with? We can call them, and you can talk to her." "I don't know who she's staying with." When he said that, he knew it was a lie, but then he told himself that it was only a little white lie, maybe little white lies weren't bad after all that has happened, and why he ran away from home. "Do you have any plans Lee?" asked Phillip, "It's dark out, where will you spend the night?" "I don't know sir I haven't found a place yet." "Have you been living up in the mountains Lee? You said you found bear in a cave in the mountains." Edith asked.

Jimmy remembered telling them that, so he would admit that much, but try not to reveal any more than he had to. "Yes ma-am, I have been living in the mountains." "Surely you haven't lived up there all your life, where did you live before going into the mountains?" "Mrs. Adams, I'm sorry, I would rather not talk about that . . . , if you don't mind . . . bear and I better go, we have imposed on your hospitality long enough, ... Thank you for feeding us, it was a wonderful meal, I'll say good ni . . ." Jimmy started to rise. "Lee," said Phillip, "You can't go up into those mountains in the dark. Stay here tonight, then tomorrow after breakfast, if you wish to leave, at least you and bear won't be hungry."

"Mr. Adams, I can't stay here, not in your home . . . you and Mrs. Adams have been very kind, I thank you for your kindness, I'll be alright." "Well then, how about sleeping in the bunkhouse?" Asked Philip. "It's empty right now!" It didn't take Jimmy long to agree to that, he didn't relish going up in those mountains at night. Phillip got a flashlight, then he Jimmy and bear headed for the bunkhouse, when they were outside Jimmy put bear down, "C'mon bear."

The next morning when Jimmy woke up, it was daylight, he didn't know what time it was, but he was so comfortable, sleeping in a real bed and not on the ground, he didn't want to get up. Bear was sleeping under the covers beside him. Not wanting to get up, but he knew he had to, sitting on the edge of the bed, he remembered Mr. Adams showing him the shower, he dug into his backpack and took out jeans, a shirt, sox and underwear.

Turning on the water, he got it as hot as he could stand, there was already soap and shampoo there, standing under the hot water felt so good, he wished it was the hot summer instead of the freezing winter. After the shower he got dressed. Then he and bear headed for the house, he didn't just walk in, he knocked again. When Mr. Adams opened the door he told Jimmy to come in. "Good morning Mr. Adams." Jimmy wiped his feet, then he and bear entered, in the kitchen, Mrs. Adams was just finishing up fixing breakfast. "Good morning Lee, did you sleep well?" asked Edith. "Yes ma-am I did, it was so comfortable I didn't want to get up!"

Mrs. Adams had prepared ham, bacon, potatoes, eggs, toast, orange juice, coffee for breakfast of course she also prepared a bowl of ham, bacon, a few potatoes and toast for bear, each of these she cut up into smaller pieces for him. Bear never had anything like that before and he dug right in and gobbled it down. While they were eating, Mr. Adams surprised Jimmy when he asked, "Lee . . . . Mrs. Adams and I were talking last night after you went to bed . . . How would you like to stay here? You could do some work, there's plenty to do, and I'll pay you a weekly wage."

Then Mrs. Adams spoke up, "Yes Lee, we would love for you to stay, it will give you time to think about what you want to do." Then it was Mr. Adams turn again, "Lee, winter is almost here, it's already cold up in those mountains, you could stay the winter, then next spring, if you feel like moving on, we'll wish you the best of luck, by then you'll have some money saved." Being surprised by their request, Jimmy just sat there dumbfounded then he asked, "What about bear, can he stay too?"

"Yes, he can stay too, but you'll have to keep a close watch on him!" Phillip was telling him, "You do realize he's a wild animal, a wolf? And wolves are a natural hunter by nature, we have chickens here, and we have had problems with wolves in the past." "Yes sir, do you mind if I think about this before I give you an answer? I'll stay and work today, by tonight, I'll have an answer."

Chapter Fifteen

Doctor Mansfield's office was down the hall from the emergency entrance waiting room. The office was for which ever doctor or doctors that was on duty. Today it is Doctor Paul Mansfield, and Doctor Larry Zimmerman. Jodie was still crying over the news that her mother had passed away, she didn't understand how that could happen, she didn't understand any medical terms, all she knew was that the doctor had just told them that her mother was gone. Just like the sheriff and Mr. Haley told them last week that Jimmy was gone. As far as she knew and could understand she lost her brother and mother in one week.

Still numb from the news, Frank stared at Dr. Mansfield, he didn't hear what he was saying, "Mr. Shannon . . . Mr. Shannon, can you tell me what your wife was doing before she was brought here?" "Huh!" "Can you tell me what your wife was doing before she was brought here?" Dr. Mansfield said again. "Oh!" While still holding Jodie, Frank told Dr. Mansfield most but not all about what has happened during the past two and a half months. He told him about Jimmy leaving, he didn't tell him why, just that he left, then about the search, finding his trail and how it ended. He also mentioned the lab report and the remarks, that they believed Jimmy to be dead. He also mentioned how Eileen had yelled and her being hysterical. Finally he told the doctor that she wanted a divorce after Jimmy's memorial service.

Doctor Mansfield understood now what probably brought on Eileen's condition, and why she was short of breath and passed out. "Mr. Shannon . . . , "Mr. Shannon," doctor Mansfield was saying, "I believe what brought on your wife's hysterical condition and why she passed out was severe trauma, from what you have told me about your son, I believe it hurt your wife most of all. You also mentioned his trail was followed to the end and that the lab report said the animal blood was either bear or wolf is that correct?" Frank wiped the tears from his eyes, "Yes doctor, that's what the lab report said." "The mind plays all kinds of tricks Mr. Shannon, when a person hears or sees something, or is being told something, no matter what, the mind registers that information. When you and your wife, was told about Jimmy, the information hit your wife harder than it did you, her mind told her how Jimmy died, the bear or a wolf. Do you understand what I'm saying?"

Frank nodded his head, he didn't want to say it out loud, neither did doctor Mansfield, that the cause of Eileen's heart stopping was the trauma she went through, it was the fact that her mind was telling her about the fight Jimmy had with a bear or wolf and lost, that his body was torn apart, shredded by claws and teeth, then possibly eaten by wild animals. Neither one wanted to say that out loud because of Jodie. After the lengthy time in Dr. Mansfield office, Jodie had simmered down, she wasn't crying, she just sat there quietly on her dads lap.

When Frank and Jodie got home, Jodie went straight up to her room, she closed the door, laid on her bed, she thought about her mother and Jimmy, how quickly they were both gone, she cried thinking about them till she fell asleep. Frank went to the phone, he called Norton warehouse, Ms. Peggy Mason answered, "Norton warehouse, Ms. Mason speaking how may I direct your call?" "Ms. Mason, It's Frank Shannon, connect me with Mr. Norton please, It's very important!" "Yes of course Mr. Shannon, I'm very sorry about your son." No one at the warehouse had yet heard about Eileen. "Thank you Ms. Mason." "Hold on please, I'll connect you to Mr. Norton's office."

When Mr. Norton answered the phone, Frank told him about Jimmy's memorial service, that it was very lovely and some of his friends told what they knew about him. He also told Mr. Norton what Mr. Middlestone had said about Jimmy. Now he had to tell Mr. Norton about Eileen. "Mr. Norton," He was going to try to say this without crying. He knew if he did cry, Mr. Norton would understand.

"Mr. Norton, what I have to tell you is going to be hard for me to say . . . I guess the only way is to come right out with it! Today Eileen passed away." "My God Frank . . . how . . . I mean how did it happen?" "It happened . . . , (sob) . . . at J . . . Jimmy's memorial service. She was telling everyone there about what had happened to Jimmy . . . (sob, sob) . . . before she fin . . . finished, she passed out, 9 . . . 911 was called, they took her to the hos . . . hos . . . hospital, she died while they were trying to save her. Dr. Mansfield said it was the trauma she went through, the pictures in her mind about Jimmy fighting with a bear or wolf. His body being torn apart and maybe eaten was too much for her. She passed out because she couldn't catch her breath she had trouble breathing on the way to the hospital. Doctor Mansfield said her heart just stopped."

"Myyyy God, I am so sorry Frank, I never in a million years would have thought, that a missing medallion would have brought all this on, I am so very sorry." "Thank you Mr. Norton, I need time off? I have to make funeral arrangements for Eileen. I don't know how long that will take." "Of course, I understand Frank take as much time as you need, don't worry about your job, we'll take care of that. Your job will be here when you are ready to return, if there's anything I can do, all you have to do is call." "Thank you Mr. Norton, your very kind. Bye sir." "Oh Frank," Mr. Norton yelled into the phone, hoping Frank heard him. "Yes sir." "Frank, please let me know when the funeral is, my wife and I will attend, and I'm sure some of the employees will too." "Yes sir, I'll keep you advised." "Thanks Frank, again, I'm truly sorry." "Thank you Mr. Norton."

After hanging up the phone, Frank just stood there thinking, a lot of thoughts ran through his mind. 'During these past two and a half months, with everything that has happened, I finally realized just how mean and strict I have really been, not only with Jimmy and Jodie, but with Eileen as well. If I had been a better husband and father, none of this would have happened.' Eileen and Jimmy would still be alive, and Jimmy would be here, at home, this is where he belongs, not up in those mountains. He was too young, too young to die, he was only ten. He sure as hell didn't deserve to die like that. This is my fault, every bit of it. Eileen is only thirty two years old, we have been married for twelve years, now she too is gone. I brought all this on, I killed them both.'

He couldn't help himself, his knees grew weak and gave way, he slid down the bottom cupboards to the floor sitting there he put his hands over his face and cried like a baby, "EILEEN . . . (sob) . . . JI . . . JIMMY . . . EILEEN, CAN YOU EVER FORGIVE ME. CAN BOTH OF YOU EVER FORGIVE ME?" Then at whisper, "I am so sorry, please forgive me."

Frank sat on the floor for a half hour crying and feeling sorry for himself, when it finally dawned on him that he and Jodie were the only two left in the house and it was up to him to take care of her. He got up went to the sink to wash his face, then went through the house looking for her, he didn't know where she was, while looking, he checked the front room, the down stairs bathroom, the garage, all around the house, the upstairs bathroom, then Jimmy's room, while checking all these places and not finding Jodie, he realized how empty and lonely the house was. When he looked in her room he saw that she was asleep, quietly he closed the door, leaving a gap of about a foot, in case she had a bad dream and woke up crying.

Chapter Sixteen

During breakfast, Jimmy asked Mr. Adams what he could do first, and what needed to be done so he wouldn't have to ask each time after he finished a job. Mr. Adams told him, "Well Lee, the stables in the barn need to be cleaned out and fresh straw laid down, there are some loose boards on the chicken coop, they can be fixed, the wire around the chicken yard is sagging in some places, the . . . "Phil, Lee can't do all that, he's just a boy!" said Edith. "Well Edith . . . ," "Excuse me," said Jimmy, "Mrs. Adams, I know I'm just a boy, and both of you have been very kind to me and bear, you have asked me to stay on through the winter, if I stay, I'll have to earn my keep."

"Lee, are you saying that you are going to stay?" asked Mrs. Adams. "I'm not sure yet." "You do know that school has started?" Edith was saying, "If you do stay, I think you should go to school, OH, you'll have a few chores to do in the morning, and some when you get home from school. Then there are the weekends, what I'm saying is, you'll have plenty of time to do the things Phil has mentioned." Jimmy didn't say anything more. The fact that Mrs. Adams brought up school, and wanted him to go, he figured the school would want to know where he went to school before. They would want to know where he lived, the town, the state, the name of the school he went to, but most of all, they would want to know his parents name's and address, as well as his full name.

In the barn there were ten horse stalls, and a door way to another room, he looked at all ten before doing anything, as Mr. Adams had said they all needed cleaning. He looked around for something to use, he saw harnesses of all kinds, a few saddles, ropes, up in the loft was hay and straw, hay on one side and straw on the other, but no tools of any kind.

The door he saw was just before the first stall on the left as he entered the barn, going through it, he saw tools of all kinds, there were also some rubber boots, too big for his feet, he decided to wear a pair anyway, with his shoes on maybe they wouldn't feel to floppy. He found a rake, a shovel and several pair of gloves. The wheel barrel was in a corner. He would start cleaning the first stall by the door. He decided to go up one side and down the other.

While he was working, he thought about what Mrs. Adams said, about him going to school, he didn't want to take that chance, not the chance of them finding out who he really is, they would call his parents, he had made up his mind, when he left home not to see or talk to them again. He did want to see Jodie he knew he couldn't see her without seeing them.

Thinking about all this while he was working, he decided to leave, he would tell Mr. and Mrs. Adams at dinner, he didn't know exactly what he was going to say. He was working on the forth stall when he stopped raking, 'How can I tell them, what can I say,' he was thinking hard, 'I could leave now, no, I can't leave now, I told them I would let them know at dinner if I was going to leave or stay. I know, I'll tell them I am leaving in the morning that I'm going to try to find my sister.'

It was late afternoon when Jimmy finished the last stall, he raked all the old straw and horse droppings out of each stall, shoveled it into the wheel barrow and took it out back, he used ten bales of fresh straw, one for each stall, when he had everything done, he rinsed all the tools and wheel barrow and put them away where he found them, when his work was done Jimmy went to the bunk house, he stripped, took a shower and changed into his last clean clothes. Having made up his mind to leave, he headed for the house to tell Mr. and Mrs. Adams. On the way he thought of his sister Jodie, wondering if she was alright.

Seeing Jodie sleeping, Frank went back down stairs, usually at this time, he would sit at the table and talk to Eileen, or he would help her prepare dinner, now she's gone, now he didn't know what to do, he went to the kitchen to start fixing dinner for him and Jodie, knowing she was asleep, he thought this was useless so he put everything away, he didn't know how long she would sleep, and he didn't want to wake her.

He just roamed from room to room, his mind in a fog, he only knew he lost his wife and son in a short period of time, and it hurt, it hurt deep down inside, it was a pain he never felt before. The more he thought about them the more he cried. Every time he walked past the stairs, he would look up to see if Jodie was there, he didn't want her to see him crying. With all these thoughts going through his mind he realized he had to call Mr. and Mrs. Garrison, Eileen's parents, and break the tragic news to them.

The phone rang and Frank hurried to the kitchen to answer it, "Hello!" "Mr. Shannon, Dr. Mansfield here, sorry to bother you, we would like to do an autopsy, to determine exactly how and why your wife died, we need your permission, also the police will get a copy of the report." "The police, what does the police have to do with this?" "Mr. Shannon, the police investigates all deaths, except those who die of natural causes. The police are saying your wife was too young to die of natural causes." Frank had seen many detective stories on TV, some were true drama stories, some were just TV programs, he had also read detective books, and knew the police looked at family members first if they suspected foul play.

"Dr. Mansfield, you have my permission, I also would like to know why, can you or will you tell me the results? when their finished." "Yes Mr. Shannon, I will let you know, and thanks, it will answer a lot of questions." "Thank you Dr. Mansfield, how long will it take?" Frank asked. "About three or four days to do the autopsy, we'll have to send all blood test's to the lab that could take a month to six weeks." Dr. Mansfield told him. "I'm going to see Mr. Watkins," said Frank, "to make the funeral arrangements. I'll let him know about the autopsy." "I understand, Mr. Watkins will call me in a few days, he always does." "Thank you, Dr. Mansfield, bye." "Bye Mr. Shannon."

As the next few days went by, Frank and Jodie didn't cry as much, oh they still had bad days, when the pain of their loss was more severe than other days, it seem to them that they were just coping with it, just getting by and enduring the pain. Frank told Jodie she should go to school on Monday, it will help her. It will help ease the pain if her mind were on her school studies. He also told her he was going back to work, that it would also help him if he kept busy. Frank was a lot nicer now, he realized just how mean and strict he was, he also realized Eileen was right, that all of what had happened was his fault, he made up his mind that he was going to changed his attitude, not only with Jodie, but with all the employees who worked for him, as well as with all the men and women who worked there. He would be more pleasant to everyone he meets.

Friday evening newspaper had the story on the front page, 'MOTHER PASSES OUT AT SONS MEMORIAL SERVICE.' Since Mr. Boyle was at the service, the whole story of Eileen's death was below the picture for all to read, by that evening the whole town knew what had happened. The next morning, being Saturday, Frank and Jodie went to Watkins funeral parlor, he talked to Mr. Watkins, made all the arrangements to have an open casket service, then have Eileen cremated. The funeral service was to be on the following Sunday. Frank called Mr. Boyle at the newspaper, he told him when the service was going to be held, he asked him to print it in the paper Leaving Watkins funeral parlor, Frank and Jodie went to the restaurant where Eileen had worked, the manager was the hostess, she showed them to a booth, then sat next to Jodie, she wanted to talk to Frank. "I read in the paper last night about Eileen, how horrible, are you alright?"

The manager, Ms. Sallie Zimmerman is a young lady, she was in her early twenties when she moved to Billings eleven years ago, she got a job at the restaurant as a waitress and worked her way up to manager, she became friends with Eileen and talked her into working there as a hostess, not a waitress. Eileen had worked there for almost five years, ever since Jodie was old enough to go to pre-school. "Yes, I'm okay!" Sallie looked at Jodie, "How about you sweetie, are you okay?" "I'm fine, I miss mommy and Jimmy!" Jodie tried hard not to cry, one tear did slide down her face, when Sallie saw it she gently wiped it away. "I know sweetie. It's hard but as time goes by you'll feel a lot better." "I hope so." Jodie replied.

After lunch Frank and Jodie return home, Jodie went up to her room, Frank went to the phone, he had to call Eileen's parents. After dialing the number he waited for someone to answer, the phone rang four times then the answering machine pick up, "Sorry we are unable to talk to you right now, please leave your number and a short message, we will return your call as soon as possible." "Mr., Mrs. Garrison, this is Frank, please call me as soon as you hear this, thank you." When Frank left his message, he spoke as calmly as he could, he didn't want to make it sound too urgent, not until he had a chance to speak to them directly.

After he hung up the phone, he just stood there, like a lost child he thought he would fix himself something to eat. 'What the hell is a matter with me,' He was thinking. 'We just had lunch, we just got home, c'mon

Frank, get a hold of yourself, your, not doing yourself or Jodie any good acting this way. you have to be strong, not only for your sake, but for Jodie as well, all this that has happened is going to be harder on her than on you, be strong for her, help her through this, you will also be helping yourself.'

Frank made a half pot of coffee, when it was ready he poured a cup, went into the front room and sat in his recliner, with the remote, he turned on the TV, tuned in the weather channel, and turned the sound down, the newscasters were talking about the high and low fronts on the east coast, it was calling for rain up and down the eastern seaboard, as far inland as the Ohio, Tennessee valleys, when they got to the west coast, they said there was a low front moving in over Washington and Oregon, it was coming down from the northwest, that the jet stream would go through northern California and across the upper half of the U.S., and that the southern winds would bring moisture, mixing with the cold air will produce rain in the lower areas, and snow, one to two feet in the mountains, along with freezing rain in some areas as the front passes through.

Frank knew from the forecast, that it would be snowing, or raining, or maybe even both in Billings Sunday night or Monday, the temperature is already cold during the day, even colder at night than usual, "It's going to be an early and hard winter this year." He said to himself. After the national weather, came the local forecast, calling for partly cloudy skies, the high in the mid to upper thirties during the day, and the night time lows in the upper teens to the lower twenty's over the weekend, rain, possible freezing rain to snow on Monday through Wednesday night, with four to six inches of snow possible, clearing on Thursday.

Jodie was still sleeping Frank was dozing in his chair when the phone rang, "Hello!" "Frank, Gene Garrison, we just got home and heard your message, we've been shopping, what's the matter? Your, voice sounded nervous or upset about something." Mr. and Mrs. Garrison lived in Memphis Tennessee. Mr. Garrison was general manager over new car sales at a local Ford dealership. During the time Jimmy was missing and they were searching for him, Eileen had called her parents and told them about it, she kept them up to date, they wanted to fly out to Billings and help in the search, Eileen told them not to, that everything was being done, she told them about Mr. Haley and Mr. Hanney.

Then they were told about the Jimmy's trail, the pictures, and the blood samples, when they had the lab report, Eileen talked to them about that also, and about the memorial service she had arranged, they wanted to fly out for the service but Eileen talked them out of it, telling them it was only a closed casket service since Jimmy wasn't there. Her parent's assured her, that if she needed them for anything all she had to do was call.

"Gene, I have terrible news, Eileen . . ." "Hold on a minute Frank, I'm putting you on speaker, I want Ruth to hear what you have to say . . . , go ahead Frank we're listening." "Gene, Ruth, yesterday afternoon, during Jimmy's memorial service, Eileen was standing in front of the congregation telling them how and why Jimmy ran away from home, when she told them about the fight everyone thinks he had with a bear or wolf, she passed out.

We called 911 and she was rushed to the hospital, Jodie and I followed. At the hospital Dr. Mansfield told us at 1:53 pm, Eileen passed away!" He heard Ruth scream, "No . . . , no . . . , no . . . , that can't be true." Frank was crying now to, he was reliving it all over again. He heard Gene sniff a few times then blow his nose. "Dr. Man . . . sniff, Mansfield said her . . . her . . . her heart j . . . j . . . just stopped, we went to his office and he asked me about J . . . J . . . Jimmy, I . . . I told him, he said the trauma that we went through was harder on her than on me, that she relived the part where Jimmy was in a fight with a bear or wolf, and lost, in her mind she could see Jimmy being torn apart, either by claws or te . . . te . . . teeth or both. It was just too much for her, and she passed out, her sub conscience took over and that's when her heart stopped, they couldn't revive her.

"Frank, why didn't you call us yesterday?" "Gene, I wasn't myself yesterday, I was hurting too much and so was Jodie, I had to take care of her, I had to try to comfort her." "Is she alright? What arrangements have you made, if any?" "Yes, Jodie is fine, I made arrangements for Eileen's funeral service for next Sunday, she wanted to be cremated, It's in her will, right now there doing an autopsy, the doctor's and police want to know why and how her heart just stopped, so do I." "I see, Ruth and I will be flying out there tomorrow, I have to arrange for time off, I will let you know." "Gene, don't come tomorrow, there is a cold front moving in, it's going to snow for the next two days, 4 to 6 inches, clearing on Thursday that would be a better day." "Alright Frank, I'll call and let you know what flight we're on, and when we'll be landing." "Thanks Gene, Jodie and I will pickup you and Ruth, see you at the airport on Thursday.

Chapter Seventeen

At the house, Jimmy didn't just walk in, he knocked, when Mr. Adams opened the door, he told Jimmy he didn't have to knock, just come in. "Thank you sir!" he said. They went to the kitchen, Mrs. Adams told them to be seated dinner was almost ready. When Jimmy sat in his chair, bear sat on the floor beside him. For dinner, Mrs. Adams fixed chicken fried steak, mashed potatoes and gravy, peas, ice tea, and corn bread, she also fixed bear a large bowl of the steak, peas, and corn bread all mixed together.

It wasn't till everyone was eating that Jimmy spoke, "Mr. and Mrs. Adams, I cleaned out all the stalls in the barn, laid down fresh straw, and put the tools away. I also want you to know, I'll be leaving in the morning. I'm taking bear back into the mountains, that's where he belongs." "Lee, winter is almost here, it will be a lot colder up there than it is here," Mr. Adams said, "Are you sure? Wouldn't you like to stay on till spring?" "yes sir, I would, but like you said, bear is a wolf, his natural instincts are of the wild, he's just a pup now, by spring he'll be full grown, he could kill your chickens, or maybe even a calf, your men are moving your cows here, aren't they?"

"Yes Lee, they are, I understand your concern, and I certainly do appreciate it, tell you what, why don't you stay a few days, it will give you a chance to rest a little, you could also work on the chicken coop, if you want, Ruth and I have to go to town to buy some supplies, we'll be gone most of the day!" "Well sir, I guess I can stay a few days." After breakfast, Jimmy went to the tool room in the barn, he got a hammer and saw, looking around he found a few slat boards and some nails. The nails he put in his coat pocket, carrying the boards, hammer a saw, he headed for the chicken coop, Mr. and Mrs. Adams was in their pick-up, as they passed Jimmy, he waved, they waved back, soon they were out of sight.

Jimmy worked all day on the chicken coop, he found the loose boards Mr. Adams mentioned, nailed them back in place, on the roof he saw some boards that were rotting, he replaced them, hammering nails here and there, measuring and cutting boards, nailing them in place. When he was done with the coop, he checked the wire around the yard, he saw where the wire was slack, thinking, he was trying to figure out, 'how can I, fix it.' Then he remembered seeing some small poles standing in the corner in the tool room.

When Mr. and Mrs. Adams returned, Jimmy and bear was sitting on the top step of the porch, he had finished his work, and had taken a warm shower, while in the shower, he called bear, and gave him a shower to. Jimmy helped carry the supplies into the house, "Mr. Adams, would you like to check the chicken coop, to see if I did okay?" Mr. Adams sensed that Jimmy wanted his approval. "Okay Lee, let's go check it out." Mr. and Mrs. Adams, was glad he asked that, for they had bought him a few presents. Mrs. Adams would take them in the house while they were gone. At the coop, Mr. Adams looked it over real good, the coop and the fence around the yard, he noticed the added boards, and the loose boards were nailed in placed, the small poles Jimmy used at the top and bottom of the wire, the wire was also pulled tight.

He turned to look at Jimmy, "You did a mighty good job Lee, looks just fine." Mr. Adams could see the pride on Jimmy's face. "Thank you Mr. Adams." Bear followed Jimmy where ever he went, being a young wolf, he acted like a young dog, Jimmy noticed this, he also knew it wouldn't last long, when bear gets older his natural instincts will take over, and he will turn into a grown wolf of the wild. Back at the house, Mrs. Adams had just put away the supplies, and was preparing dinner. The dinner is beef stew, with a salad, and strawberry short cake for dessert. While the stew was heating, Mrs. Adams suggested, "Let's go in the front room, it will take a while for the stew to heat up."

Jimmy sat on the couch, Ruth and Phil went down the hall, Jimmy had no idea why, a few minutes later when they entered the front room, Ruth was carrying several packages, and Phil was carrying two long boxes, they placed them in front of Jimmy. Jimmy looked up at them with a look of wonderment on his face, "These are for you Lee." Ruth said. "For me, I don't understand." "Well Lee," said Phil, "You've been here two days, and you did two day's work, so I owe you two day's pay, and since your leaving tomorrow, we thought you could use these." "Open them." Ruth said.

Jimmy opened the first one, it was three pair of woolen sox and three flannel shirts, the second package was a new lined winter coat with a hood, the next was a long skinny box, when he opened it, it totally surprised him, it was a brand new bow made of fiberglass and polyurethane, there was also a new quiver, a little bigger than the one he made.

The bow was four and a half feet long. Jimmy strung the bow he wanted to see how strong it was, with his left arm straight, it took all his strength to pull the string back to his chin. It was a good bow. The last package he opened was two dozen arrows, six were target arrows, and eighteen were hunting arrows, the arrow heads were three sided with razor sharp edges. He looked at both of them, "Mr., Mrs. Adams, I don't know what to say." "You don't have to say anything Lee," Ruth told him, "We were happy to do it." "That's right Lee, besides, these things will help you and bear up in those mountains." Phil added.

Jimmy gave them both a hug as he thanked them. "Lee if you want, you can leave the bow and arrows that you made here now that you have these new ones." "No sir, Mr. Adams, I'm going to take them with me, as a backup, I may never need them, but just in case." "I understand." "I'll go fix dinner," Ruth said, "Phil, come with me, you can set the table." After dinner, the three of them sat at the table, Ruth and Phil had coffee, Jimmy was drinking water, bear had eaten all his dinner and was now sitting on Jimmy's lap.

The conversation was Mr. and Mrs. Adams asking him questions about where he was going and what he was going to do? "Lee, you do realize that it won't be long before the snow flies." Mr. Adams stated. "Especially up on those mountain tops." "Yes sir, I know, bear and I have already been in snow, we got stuck on top of a mountain for two days before it stopped snowing, bear and I went off the mountain, I found a nice warm valley, that was a few weeks ago."

Jimmy didn't want to tell them exactly where he was going, or what direction, he also didn't want to lie. He wasn't going to lie. He just said, "I really don't know yet, but I'll be going that way." He pointed west, that was the way he came down off the mountains, that's the way he'll start out tomorrow, once he gets up in the mountains, and out of sight, he'll turn south.

Lying in bed that night, his thoughts were about Mr. and Mrs. Adams, 'what wonderful people they are, and how much he would like to stay there for the winter, but he knew he couldn't, he couldn't because of the questions they asked. He figured they were normal questions from people who didn't know him, who just wanted to help him, but then again, they might want that information to tell the police, they might have told the police already, when they were in town today. They might be coming after him tonight, or be here first thing in the morning, what should I do.'

Earlier in the day after his work was done and after his shower, he washed his dirty clothes, hung them in the bunk house to dry since he was leaving in the morning. Before lying down, he folded his clothes and packed his backpack, with three more shirts and sox and two winter coats he had to fold his cloths as small and tight as he could. He decided to wear his old coat when he left, saving the new one for when it was really cold. He could wrap bear up in the old one. He also filled all four plastic water bottles he had and packed them in his backpack. Lying there all covered up and warm with his thoughts, he fell asleep.

It was shortly after 10 pm when he got into bed. He and bear was warm, comfortable, and sleeping soundly, all of a sudden bear raised up and growled softly, his movement woke Jimmy, "What's the matter bear?" he whispered, bear growled softly again. He didn't know how long he was asleep or what time it was, slowly and as quietly as he could he got out of bed, went to the only window in the bunk house, looking out he could see the main house, he saw Mr. Adams pick-up, on the other side of the pick-up, he saw another vehicle, he couldn't tell what kind it was, and he couldn't see anyone walking around, it was too dark, even though the sky was clear, there was no moon.

He kept watching, when the front door opened, he could see two men and two woman, from the light inside the house he could tell two of the people he knew was Mr. and Mrs. Adams, he didn't know who the other two were. When the other lady moved, he saw the badge on her shirt, it gleamed from the light inside. "Bear," he said, "That's the law, Mr. and Mrs. Adams had to of told them I was here, they came to get me, we have to leave, and leave now." He put on his old coat his backpack, both quivers of arrows, one on each side. With both bows in his left hand he slowly opened the door, "Shhhh . . . Shhhhh," he whispered to bear, leaving the door open, he crouched down, keeping an eye on the house, he made his way around to the nearest side, out of sight of the house, he stood up and went to the far side of the bunk house, peeking around the corner, he could still see all four of them on the porch.

Keeping an eye on the house, he looked around for cover he could use, the only cover near to him was the chicken coop, it was at least one hundred and fifty feet away, looking back at the house, he figured this was his best chance, the people on the porch wasn't looking his way, he picked bear up, "Shhhh," he whispered. Crouched down, he moved slowly, trying not to attract their attention. He reached the coop safely, then whispered to bear again, "Shhhh . . . . Shhhh," bear sensed what was happening, he didn't make a sound. Since it was the middle of the night, the chickens were in the coop, he guessed they were trying to sleep and stay warm, they also didn't make any noise.

Watching the house, Jimmy saw the two police officers go down the steps, with flashlights on, they heading for the bunk house he looked back to the house and saw the front door close. As the officers got closer to the bunk house he started backing away keeping the coop between them, just like he did with the jeep up in the mountains when he took the picnic basket. Then he started running, he ran past the house and headed toward the mountain, the same mountain he was on when he spotted the ranch. Approaching the first knoll, Jimmy had a good head start on the officers, he heard someone yell, "STOP, YOU THERE, LEE STOP." Then it was a woman's voice, "LEE, STOP RUNNING, WE'RE NOT GOING TO HARM YOU, WE JUST WANT TO TALK TO YOU, PLEASE STOP." He paid no attention to them, he kept running.

Reaching the barbed wire fence, he put bear down, he didn't bother trying to go through the fence, he held onto a post and climbed over, on the other side, he and bear disappeared among the trees, he worked his way around trees and bushes, a few bushes he went through, finally he stopped, he was out of breath. He sat down, bear sat beside him, he petted bear while watching the house, what he could see of it. Off to his left, the same place where he climbed the fence, he saw two shadows headed back toward the house, figuring they were the police, he relaxed they didn't catch him.

Sitting there thinking, he wondered what Mr. and Mrs. Adams told them, it couldn't be much, he really didn't tell them much about himself, they don't know his full name, and they don't know where his family lives, even if they find out about him it don't matter, he's back in the mountains, here he can hide from anyone who comes looking. Now he had to find someplace to stay the rest of the night, "Well bear, looks like we're on our own again," he said, "You want to go to the top and stay there the rest of the night?" Bear let out a low growl. "I agree bear we'll keep walking, come morning we'll find someplace to sleep."

All through the rest of the night they walked and rested, Jimmy didn't know which way they were heading, North, South, or West, he got turned around so many times, one thing he did know it wasn't East, come morning he would know, if the sun shone, If not, he would figure it out. When morning did come and the sun peeked over the eastern mountains, he looked up at the sky, it was partly cloudy, 'no rain or snow today,' he thought, now to find a place to sleep. Keeping the sun to his left, he knew he was going south, still on the side of a mountain, the slope wasn't as steep as the other mountains he was on. Easing his way down he hoped to find a place.

At the bottom, he looked around, even though it was flat, it was heavily wooded, he searched this way and that way, what he found was another hole in the ground, or another wolf den, it didn't matter, he and bear were tired, checking it out, he found it empty, it was as big as the other one was where he fought and killed the bear, he hoped he didn't have to do that again. He and bear entered the hole, he told bear to stay there, after unloading what he was carrying, he went to find some branches to cover the entrance like before, he found some thick dead branches and some small logs, dragging these, he covered the hole, it was hard putting them in place securely, so he thought it would be hard for any animal to get in.

He made up their bed with the rain coat, bear and deer skins and blanket he put on his new winter coat, made a bed for bear with his old coat next to him. Jimmy sat there for a long time same as before, he listened to the sounds, peeked through the cracks of the branches he had placed at the entrance. Not seeing anything and only hearing the wind, he was satisfied, bear was already asleep, so he layed down, covered up, and soon was fast asleep, his last thoughts were about Jodie, he wondered how she was.

Chapter Eighteen

Frank had called Jodie's school and told them that she would be out of school for a few days, he explained the reason why. Today was her second day back to school and it seemed to help. Now with her grandparents coming here, it might help keep her mind occupied with other thoughts even more. Frank and Jodie met Mr. and Mrs. Garrison at the airport, their flight landed at five twenty pm, the airport was of medium size, it wasn't one of those big international airports. When Jodie saw Mr. and Mrs. Garrison walking toward them, she took off running, "GRANDMA, GRANDPA", she yelled, she and Jimmy both loved their grandparents, she hugged them both they in turn hugged her.

Frank shook hands with Bud Garrison, and he hugged Abby Garrison, on the way to the house they talked about the flight, and the weather in Memphis. Since Frank was doing most of the talking, Bud and Abby assumed he didn't want to talk about Eileen in front of Jodie, so they wouldn't push the issue, they would wait till after Jodie went to bed. "Are you hungry?" Frank asked them, "We can stop for dinner, or I can fix something at home, but I must warn you, I'm not a very good cook, I still have a lot to learn!" They decided to stop.

At the house, Frank helped carry their suitcases up to their room, the last two day's he kept busy cleaning, dusting, polishing the furniture, swept and waxed the kitchen floor, change bedding on all beds, did the laundry. At eight thirty, he ran Jodie's bath water, Abby helped her bathe. Then tucked her into bed, Jodie talked about her mother, asking questions, at seven years old she didn't understand why her mother had died. Abby tried her best to explain, even though she herself didn't quite understand and was hurting for the loss of her daughter. Abby stayed with Jodie awhile longer, gently rubbing her head, when she was asleep, Abby went down stairs.

In the front room, Frank and Bud were sitting, talking about other things, they were waiting for Abby before he told them what had happened. When she was seated, he told them everything, about the medallion, Jimmy's leaving, and why, the search, and what Mr. Haley and Mr. Hanney found, up to the funeral service, and the doctors diagnoses that the trauma was too much for Eileen to handle, and her heart just stopped, they couldn't revive her. Also they were waiting for the autopsy report, and Eileen's wish to be cremated, that all the arrangements have been made. When he was done, he asked them if they would like to see the pictures, of course they said no.

On Saturday evening, all of Eileen's friends, and people she hardly knew, as well as Frank's, came to the viewing, as was reported in the paper, even Mr. Middlestone, Mr. Haley, Mr. Hanney and their families, as well as others from the tribe were there. Sheriff John Macklin and his family were also at the service. The top half of the coffin was open, showing her from the waist up. It was satin white with gold and silver trim. Seeing Eileen lying there in her coffin, dressed in a white gown, very little make up, forearms folded across her chest, her fingers interlocked, holding a single red rose. Jodie cried uncontrollably, she yelled, "MOMMY, WHY DID YOU HAVE TO DIE? PLEASE COME BACK, I LOVE YOU, I DON'T WANT YOU TO LEAVE US, PLEASE MOMMY!" Frank had to take Jodie outside, he tried to calm her down, holding her tight, they both cried. The ladies who knew her also wept when they saw her, some of the men had tears in their eyes. She was too young, too young for this to happen.

Her parents, Bud and Abigail Garrison wept the hardest they stood at the casket looking down at their daughter with tears pouring from their eyes. That afternoon, they knew one of them, Frank, Bud, or Abby was to give a eulogy about her, but neither one thought they could, not without breaking down. Frank suggested they each write what they wanted to say and he would ask Mr. Haley too read them. "NO," Bud said, "She's our daughter, and your wife, we will give the eulogy, no matter how hard it is.

When the service was over, as the people left, they shook hands with Frank, Mr. and Mrs. Garrison, frank was holding Jodie and they acknowledged her as well. After everyone departed, they went home, it was a somber night, everyone was sad, eyes red, Mrs. Garrison had a headache and retired, Jodie went to her room and closed the door. Frank and Bud sat in the front room, "Frank," said Bud, "We'll be leaving in the morning, how are you set? Are things alright with you?" "Yes Bud, everything's fine, why do you ask?" "Well, Abby and I have talked about this, and we would like for Jodie to come home with us, back to Memphis, right now she needs a woman in her life. Abby can help her get through this. We'll see to it she goes to school, and she has whatever she needs. Besides, you have to work, and take care of things here."

"I don't know Bud, you're asking me to give up the only family I have left, what would I do here by myself, without Jodie?" "Frank, you have think about Jodie's welfare, what's best for her, Do you really think you can take good care of her and still do your job, from what you and Eileen have told us, your job is very demanding, you sometimes bring your work home, the paperwork, Eileen has told us that you have even worked late into the night, Frank, we just want what's best for Jodie, this is harder on her than it is the rest of us, she's only seven!"

"I don't know Bud!" "Well Frank, I'm going to retire for the night, think about it, we can talk in the morning, good night." The next morning, the others were eating breakfast when Frank entered the kitchen, he poured a cup of coffee and sat at the table, Abby asked him what he wanted for breakfast, "Nothing to eat, just coffee, thanks." He answered. Then he turned to look at Jodie, "Jodie, grandma and grandpa are leaving today, their plane leaves this evening, and they would like to know if you would like to go home with them?" Jodie looked at her dad, she looked surprised. "You mean go with them on an airplane, to their house?" she asked. "Yes, grandpa and I talked about it last night. If you want to go, you can, you and grandma can pack two suitcases later I'll call the airport and arrange a ticket for you. Do you want to go?"

Jodie remembers her grandparent's house from the vacation they all went on last summer. Eileen and Frank took a two week vacation at the same time and flew to Memphis with Jimmy and Jodie. She liked her grandparent's house, and she liked the hot summer days and cool nights, in Montana the days were nice, but the nights were a lot colder than at her grandma's house. "Yes, I would like to go to grandma's house." When she said this, she also thought of what Jimmy had told her, the afternoon he left home. 'Be careful around mom and dad, watch what you say and do, you know dad is mean and my leaving might make it worse for you.'

"Alright Jodie, I will call the airline and buy you a ticket." That evening at the airport Frank said goodbye to Bud and Abby, he hugged Jodie and told her to be good for her grandparents he would call her soon. Watching them board the plane, he waved, they waved back. Frank stayed and watched the plane take off. When he returned home he stood just inside the front door, looking around he thought, 'Here I am in this big house all alone, my wife and son are gone, my daughter wants to stay with her grandparents, not me. I just lost all of my family.' Frank went to sofa in the living room, laid down and cried.

Chapter Nineteen

Since there was no lightning and thunder Jimmy slept soundly thru the night. At morning twilight he awoke, he just laid there, eyes open and listening for any strange sound or any sound other than the wind. He heard none, only the wind whispering through the trees. Sitting up, he looked through the cracks of the block cade, searching for any kind movement he studied the area he could see long and hard, the only thing moving were the branches of the trees, bushes and tall grass. The morning air was cold, a lot colder, he knew it was fall and would soon snow, especially in the mountains. He knew this from watching the weather report with his dad.

Using his foot he kicked one of the logs knocking it free, the small log rolled down the hill a ways, that's when he heard a low growling sound, he stiffened, sat very still, he heard the growl again that seemed to be off too his right, it was a different growl, not a low deep growl like a bear, like the one he had the fight with, it has a higher pitch. 'It must be a wolf and this is his den, I wonder how many are out there. I don't want to fight a wolf or wolves this early. I may not have a choice.' He thought 'I don't have a choice.' He decided then to change coats he didn't want to ruin the new one, strapping the bowie knife to his right leg he noticed his hands shaking. At this moment he wasn't thinking about food or water, only one thought was going through his mind 'I'm scared, I don't want to do this, if there is more than one I'm going to die, I might die anyway, one thing I do know is I can't stay here.' Taking the Bowie knife in hand, he kicked the rest of the block cade away. On hands and knees he slowly exited the cave looking first left then right, he didn't realize it but tears were escaping his eyes and running down his face. Not seeing any wolves he stopped to scan the area all around. Back and forth his eyes went searching every tree, bush and rock, he even watched the movement of the grass to see if anything moved or of any discoloration. Then he heard that low growl again, this time it was above him, higher up on the mountain.

On hands and knees with the knife in his right hand he listened, he concentrated on what was above him, closing his eyes he blocked out everything in his mind except that low growl, now he was ready, as ready as he could be. 'This is it, it's now or never' he thought, Jimmy stood up and turned around as quickly as he could only to face a full grown cougar perched on a boulder about ten feet above him. Looking at the cougar eye to eye Jimmy waited, the next move was up to the big cat. He was hoping it would leave. Jimmy stared at the cat intensely.

Now Jimmy was really scared, his whole body was shaking, never having been in this situation before or seeing something like this on TV and what to do, he just stood there looking up. He waited, not taking eyes off the cat, at this moment a thousand things were running through his mind, 'I can't run, the cougar can run faster than me, if I step aside when he jumps he'll just turn and come after me, no, the only thing I can do is stand still and maybe he will go away.' The cougar didn't go away, Jimmy watched it crouch down, getting ready to leap. Scared to death Jimmy just stood there looking at the mountain lion the knife in his right, he was shaking knowing this was his last day on earth, he was going to die.

Just then the cougar leaped at Jimmy, not knowing what to do he raised his right arm, holding the knife tight and his eyes closed as he took a large step forward. As the cougar passed over Jimmy's head he was impaled on the knife and it cut the cougar's stomach open. The big cat let out a loud scream as it hit the ground rolled downhill, his insides exiting from the force of the impact and the momentum of rolling downhill. Jimmy was knocked to the ground by the cougar and hit his forehead on a rock, it didn't knock him out but it did stun him and made him dizzy. When Jimmy sat up he looked around, not seeing the cat he got to his feet hoping this was over. The movement of getting up shot pain through the left side of Jimmy's chest and left shoulder.

Jimmy wasn't concerned with the pain right at this moment, he was more concerned about the cougar, where is he, is he dead or did he run off. Jimmy had to know the answers, with knife in hand he started searching, after a few steps down hill Jimmy saw the big cat lying at the base of a bush. The cat was not moving, Jimmy could see that its stomach had been cut open. Looking all around he saw the cat's guts and blood from where it landed to where it now laid.

Being careful and not wanting to get too close to the cougar until he knew it was dead Jimmy picked up a rock, he threw it and hit the cat in the rib area, there was no movement. Slowly Jimmy circled around to his right keeping an eye on the cat for any kind of movement. Coming up behind the cougar, Jimmy picked up another rock and threw it at the cat's head the rock just grazed the big cat between its ears. Still the cat didn't move. Dropping the knife and quickly put his left knee on the cat's neck, Jimmy got hold of the front leg then with his right hand and as fast as he could Jimmy reached in the cat's chest grabbed his heart and pulled as hard as he could. Holding the heart in his hand, Jimmy now knew the cat was dead, it was at this moment that the pain he had hit home.

Looking at his coat, Jimmy saw it was blood soaked. Dropping the heart, Jimmy picked up his knife and making his way back to the cave, he sat down and checked on bear, bear just sat there looking at him, with his right hand Jimmy made the motion for him to stay. Bear had grown considerable since Jimmy found him, at first Jimmy would talk to bear, but it has been months since Jimmy has spoken out loud, all his talking to bear was with hand motions since bear couldn't talk back.

Very slowly and painfully Jimmy removed his coat, that's when he saw the cut's, the claw marks the cat gave him when he leaped from the rock and was over head. 'Somehow the cougar scratched me, probably with one of his hind legs as he was falling. I have to get off the side of this mountain, down in a valley somewhere where there is water. Its winter now and the snow will be flying soon.' These were the thoughts going through Jimmy's mind as he took off this shirt. Cutting the sleeve off, he folded it for a bandage, placing it over his wounds, he took what was left of his string and wrapped around his chest and shoulder to hold the bandage in place. After putting his coat on Jimmy just sat there for a long time thinking about what has just happened, 'I a boy who is only ten years old just killed a mountain lion with my knife, I have to admit it was only pure luck, I knew I had no chance, that today I was going to die.' Looking up at the sky, he closed his eyes and thanked God for protecting him. Gathering up what he had, motioning for bear to follow they headed south making their way down off the mountain.

The going was slow, carrying what he had in his left hand and over his shoulder despite the pain, Jimmy had to use his right hand to hold on to bushes or tree limbs and rocks. Reaching the valley floor he looked around, no water of any kind, not a creek or even a small water hole. It was midmorning when Jimmy and bear started across the small valley heading south.

Bear was running around, he went this way and that way, sniffing the ground from time to time bear would stop look back to see where Jimmy was then continue on. Even through his pain Jimmy had to smile at what bear was doing, like he was hunting for something, bear isn't a little pup anymore, it's been how long since I found him, I don't remember, I don't even know what day or month this is. Then Jimmy realized bear was hunting so when bear stopped so did Jimmy.

It didn't take long when all of a sudden bear took off running, zig zagging every which way, Jimmy just stood there he could tell where bear was by the way the tall dead grass moved, sure, the wind blew and the grass would wave but not like this. Just as quick as it started it stopped. Jimmy guessed bear to be forty or fifty yards in front of him, waiting to see what was going to happen next Jimmy gripped the knife handle just in case.

Within a few minutes bear came back with a rabbit in his mouth, squatting down Jimmy smiled and petted bear then gently scratched him behind his ears, bear dropped the rabbit his tail just a waggling for he knew his master was proud of him. Sitting on the ground Jimmy took out his knife, he gutted the rabbit then cut slits in both hind legs to carry the rabbit on his belt. He decided to skin it later, right now he had to find water to clean his wounds. He touched his forehead, it was sore but not bleeding, he wondered if his shoulder was still bleeding or not, he couldn't feel anything sliding down his arm.

When Jimmy and bear reached the other side of the small valley, he realized they were still pretty high up on the mountain side. All he knew was it would be getting dark soon enough and he had to find a place to spend the night.

Same as before they started downhill, Jimmy only using his right hand to hold on to things. It was slow going but Bear stayed by his side carefully watching, making sure everything was all right. Bear loved

Jimmy, Jimmy always treated him with love and kindness, during the few months that they have been together bear has also learned to trust Jimmy. Coming to a bluff Jimmy looked all around, all he saw was more mountains. It was early afternoon now and cold, the wind was blowing and from where he was standing made the cold air freezing.

It wasn't until he was ready to look for a way down that he saw it, a clearing, staring through the trees trying to see how big it was, he couldn't really tell, from where he was it looked like another small one. Something else he couldn't see was water. It took several hours to reach the clearing, but when they got there Jimmy saw that it wasn't a small clearing but a huge valley surrounded by mountains and all kinds of trees, pine, maple, spruce and some oak but most of all there was water. At first he didn't see the water but he could hear it.

Making his way toward the sound of running water Jimmy did finally see it, a small creek running down off the mountain. Standing on the bank by the water's edge Jimmy now had to find a safe place to spend the night, he knew the night was going to be cold but not as cold as last night high up on the mountain side. It was getting late in the day he decided to find something, anything where he and bear would be safe then he would tend to his wounds and skin the rabbit bear caught, hoping to get all this done before dark, plus he still had to gather wood for a fire. He knew bear was starving as was he. The rabbit will taste good once it's cooked.

Crossing the creek, Jimmy started looking for another wolf den, not finding one he kept looking. What he did find was a very small cluster of rocks and boulders, there was no cave but with a little work and some sticks or small logs he could make a place and with a fire it should be a lot warmer.

Walking around he found where some trees had fallen, some had fallen recently others had fallen a long time ago and were dried out, these are the ones he would use, they would be lighter. It was dark when he finished, looking at it he thought 'It isn't much but it will have to do, tomorrow I will find something better or fix this one up better'.

The next morning Jimmy woke up at dawn, he laid there as he always did listening for any strange sound. He heard nothing, only the wind blowing through the trees. When he and bear came out of their make shift cave Jimmy looked all around to see if he could see any wild animals, what he did see surprised him, two deer on the other side of the valley drinking water, he also saw a few rabbits, coming down off the mountain further down the valley were three grown wolves making their way toward the water, Jimmy also saw flocks of birds, he didn't know what kind they were but they were all trying to get a drink of water.

As he and bear stood there together watching the animals he realized it wasn't really that cold, not yet anyway, soon the snow will come and it will be freezing. Standing there taking in all his surroundings he thought 'I don't want to get caught out in the open when it does snow, that's what animal planet said on TV, so, this here valley is where bear and I will spend the winter, come spring we will head south again. Now I have to find some place for bear and I to sleep, but first I set my snares and hope to catch something before dark.'

After setting his snares Jimmy and bear walked south searching for a place to sleep, they hadn't gone more than a hundred feet when bear stopped turned toward the side of the mountain and growled in a low tone, hearing this Jimmy also stopped he looked at bear then looked the way bear was looking, he stood still slowly pulling his knife out getting ready to fight whatever bear was growling at. Standing there beside bear Jimmy stood motionless only his eyes moved, he searched the side of the mountain looking, listening for any sound or movement, he saw and heard none.

Slowly with knife in hand Jimmy made his way up the slope and into the trees, bear being just ahead of him, they made their way very slowly being careful not to make any noise. Twenty five feet up the slope in the thicket of bushes and trees bear stopped as did Jimmy, what they saw was a hole in the side of the mountain, 'Another wolf den or maybe a bears den, it also could be empty, no animal at all using it, I need to check it out.'

Slowly and carefully Jimmy moved toward the opening, he could smell the odor of an animal or animals, when he reached the opening he stood to one side, bear hadn't moved he was poised ready to run and jump at whatever came out, he was ready to fight. Jimmy waited, listening for a sound, a sound of any kind but he heard none. Looking into the hole was dark, he knew if he entered and there was a wolf or bear in there he wouldn't stand a chance, he had to have a torch. He decided to leave and check it out tomorrow.

For the next few weeks Jimmy not only found a place to sleep but was able to catch rabbits in his snares plus he killed a deer with his new bow and arrows. The present time was good for Jimmy and bear, with plenty to eat and drink, the weather had turned warm, it was still cold at night but the days Jimmy remembered were like Indian summer. During this time his wounds also healed. For the first time in months he was able to be a boy again. He didn't know where he was, for that matter he didn't even know what day or month this was and he didn't care, he and bear ran up and down the valley jumped over fallen trees, wrestled with each other, Jimmy laughed and bear howled.